Winter Wonder

A Lennox in Love Novella

TINA MARTIN

Copyright © 2019 Tina Martin

WINTER WONDER

ISBN:

Inquiries? Contact:
tinamartinbooks@gmail.com

Visit **Tina Martin Publications** at:
www.tinamartin.net

Winter Wonder, A Lennox in Love Novella – Synopsis

A winter launch party.

A shy entrepreneur.

A jealous best friend..?

One smokin' hot Lennox!

Drake Lennox, maintenance manager for Lennox Enterprises' network of hotels and resorts, spends most of his time working – and by working, that entails managing his team. He doesn't take maintenance calls but does so as a favor for his cousin Joelle Lennox at Smoky Mountain Lodge. There, he meets Lavina Nelson – a representative for Mountain View Beauty who's organizing a grand launch party for her latest beauty products. Drake insists upon helping her set up the banquet room and discovers the businesswoman has more stake in the company than she leads on. She's passionate about her work but prefers to stay in the background with her best friend happily taking the lead and spotlight.

Can he help reclaim what's rightfully hers?

Praise for the Lennox in Love Series:

"Loved It. I read *Claiming You* and Remy and Emmie were amazing together. I'm rereading *Claiming You* now. Loved their connection and how they were destined for each other." – Reader review of *Caught in the Storm with a Lennox*

"*Claiming You* was a great read could not put it down until I was done. I loved the chemistry between Emory McNeil and Remington Lennox. Tina Martin job well done...you always write books that pull at the heart strings." – Reader review of *Claiming You*

"The much anticipated story for Giovanni Lennox was just what the doctor ordered, a heavy dosage of laughter, emotional issues, and loves unbounded connection between an unlikely pair." – Reader review of *Making You My Business*

"The Lennox series is easy to read and fun. This story takes you through the eye-opening experience of acknowledging a love that was there all the time." – Reader Review of *Wishing That I Was Yours*

"I absolutely loved this book. I stayed up until three in the morning trying to finish it. The story is so timeless. And it actually helps you learn a lesson. Don't rush someone – don't rush yourself into something that can impact your entire life." – Reader review of *Before You Say I Do*

TINA MARTIN

WINTER WONDER
A Lennox in Love Novella, Book 5

Chapter 1

Drake Lennox got out of his black GMC work truck, zipped up a dark blue pair of overalls and decided which toolbox he needed for this particular job – a job he wasn't supposed to be on. Joelle, his cousin by marriage and the ever-efficient manager of Smoky Mountain Lodge, had called him first thing this morning. She needed a light in the women's lobby bathroom changed since the thing was flickering faster than a strobe light in a backwoods juke joint – the kind that sells moonshine and plays songs by Joe Tex. Drake oversaw all maintenance operations for Lennox

Enterprises. Under normal circumstances, he'd dispatch one of his workers but unfortunately they were all out on job assignments. With Joelle being who Joelle was, there was no way she'd wait for two hours, let alone two days for someone to come out and repair the light. So, he took it upon himself to do it – going above and beyond the call of duty to keep their properties up to par. He – no *they* – had a reputation to uphold. The Lennox properties of resorts and hotels were the best around. They needed to stay that way.

As he was getting his tools together, his phone rang. Joelle's name came up on the screen. He answered, "If you don't calm down girl, I'ma call Giovanni on you. Goodness gracious."

Joelle laughed. "I *am* calm, thank you very much. I was calling to see where you were."

"Like I said, I'm calling Vanni. You—boy oh, boy—I see he got his hands full with your lil' smart mouth."

"Hush. Where are you?"

"I'm outside, girl, in the parking lot 'bout to break my neck on a patch of ice." He wiggled his fingers into a pair of black work gloves. "Nobody plowed the lot this morning?" he asked, looking around. It looked like a plow had been through at some point over the weekend – piles of dirty snow was pushed to the parking lot's edge. It wasn't a good look, but when you lived in the mountains, this was to be expected. Snow – and lots of it.

"They *did* plow it, but it snowed again and the temperature is steadily dropping. I told them to come back later and put down some salt."

"Good. It's about to be a skating rink out this piece." He closed the toolbox and put the tailgate back up on his truck. "You wanna know what has me curious this morning, Jo?"

"What?"

"Why is it that every time something goes wrong *here*, it's an emergency?"

"Because my location has to run smoothly. Need I remind you Smoky Mountain Lodge is the top-grossing hotel under Lennox Enterprises thanks to *yours truly*?"

"Can't argue with you there, but still everything isn't an emergency."

"I beg to differ. I have VIP guests today."

"Who do you have coming in?"

"Aleeta Cofield from Mountain View Beauty."

"I know who she is," he mumbled.

"Oh, do you now?"

"Yep. What time is she supposed to be here?"

"Any minute now, hence my *emergency*."

"Ah'ight. I'll be there in a moment."

He put his phone in the right pocket of the overalls then walk-skated across the parking lot. He couldn't let Aleeta Cofield of all people see him dressed in a maintenance uniform. He wasn't knocking the hustle, but he'd worked his tail off to earn the manager position. He was proud to be a manager – rocking his Brooks

Brothers suits and overpriced leather shoes. And Aleeta – she was a woman about her business. A woman who'd been on national TV showcasing her beauty products, services, beauty tips and tutorials. She was the ultimate come-up story. He'd heard she started the business in her kitchen and now her products were being used by celebrities.

Her time was limited.

He found that out the last time he tried to talk to her. She had a beauty summit at one of their other hotels this past summer. He was filling in that day too, wearing the blue overalls to protect his clothing. He tried to talk to her then, but she'd looked him up and down like he stank. She shook his hand, surprisingly. That told him Aleeta didn't deal with men who weren't on her level professionally. Blue-collar men didn't have a chance of getting her attention.

Today, if he worked fast enough, she wouldn't see him in overalls. She'd see him in a suit – what he wore on a daily basis to work. Maybe if she saw the businessman side of him, she'd give him the time of day or at least be unpretentiously cordial. Maybe.

Drake walked in, stomped snow and salt off his Timbs on the large rug at the door then waved at Joelle as he passed through the lobby. Joelle threw up a finger trying to get his attention while she was on the phone, but he kept on walking toward the bathroom in question.

"Hey, Drake," he heard Joelle shout from the reservation desk.

"I got it, Jo," he told her. When he reached the women's bathroom, he tapped on the door and slowly pushed it open to check if anyone was inside and once he confirmed no one was there, he went in and roped off the entrance to make sure no one entered while he worked. The blinking light was playing with his eyes. It was one of the fancy scone-style wall lamps between one of the mirrors above the sinks.

"Well, aren't you annoying," he said to the light. "If I don't get you out of here, Jojo will have an aneurysm. Do you know that?" He took a flat-head screwdriver from the toolbox and unworked four screws to remove the lampshade. That's when he heard a toilet flush.

He spun around.

What the...

Someone was in one of the stalls. Either that or this place was haunted. Most likely, though, it was a chick...

It was.

A woman.

Aleeta-freakin'-Cofield of all people...

She screamed upon stepping out of the stall. Screamed like she was about to be stabbed. Or like somebody was running behind her wearing a Jason mask. Or like a black bear just took a swipe at her, or more apropos in her case, like she just discovered she had a pimple the day of a photoshoot.

Drake frowned and threw his hands up like he was being approached by a racist state trooper. "Hands up, don't shoot," he said to boot.

"What are you doing in here?" she yelled after pulling the earphones from her ear.

"Calm down, woman," he said to her. She was clearly distraught. Any wrong moves by him and she was probably dialing 911 and he really would find himself in a hands-up-don't-shoot situation.

"Don't tell me to calm down," she said. "What are you doing in here?"

Amused, Drake said, "Presenting..." He gestured to the light and the lampshade. "In case you think two plus two equals five, I'm fixing the light."

She rolled her eyes. "Well, you could have knocked and let somebody know you were in here. Dang."

"I *did* knock. You had your earphones in. By the way, who listens to music while they're in the middle of taking a dump?"

"*Ugh.* You're disgusting. I wasn't taking a dump."

"So you expect me to believe it took you ten minutes to pee. Ten whole minutes..."

"OMG—I don't care what you believe," she said. Her face was twisted up something awful. She was normally a pretty girl, but somebody should warn her to never make that face. That *somebody* was him.

"You shouldn't make that face. You look like a newborn pitbull puppy."

"And you look like a fool." She shook her

head. "Why am I even entertaining this nonsense?"

"You need to be asking yourself why you're wearing earphones, listening to music in a public bathroom."

"Well, aren't you simple-minded to think that just because someone is wearing earphones, they *must* be listening to music. It's an audiobook." Then she mumbled, "Something that might interest you since you probably can't read..."

"I hope it's one on manners," he said.

Her eyes rolled again. "I have manners."

"No, you do not," Drake said shaking his head. "Maybe when you were like seven, but as an adult, let me be the first to tell you—you're a rude piece of something..."

"*Ugh*...stop talking to me."

Drake smirked, shook his head and continued with removing the lightbulb.

"Excuse me?" she said.

Through the mirror, he saw the moment she cocked her head to one side and threw her hand on her hip. He continued working when he heard her snap her fingers.

Twice.

He stopped, looked at her.

"Aren't you going to give me some privacy?" she asked, her arms still crossed and she had the nerve to bounce as if the motion would set a fire beneath him.

"Oh, you want me to talk now," Drake said. "Do I have your permission to speak?"

She huffed. Her eyes made a half circle yet

again.

"If you keep on rolling your eyes like that, those fake lashes coming smooth off. And, newsflash—you don't need privacy to wash your hands."

"This is women's restroom!" she reminded him as if that was needed to be stated.

"You're a bright one, aren't you? You're right. This *is* a women's restroom. Those audiobooks are paying off. What exactly were you listening too, anyway? You look like the kind of chick who'd listen to an audiobook about audiobooks."

Drake chuckled. He couldn't believe he'd actually entertained the thought of talking to her the last time he saw her. She was a pretty girl, but butt-ugly if you factored in her personality. If she was really *this* rude, he wasn't about to be courteous.

She was still pouting when he said, "Those dirty hands won't wash themselves."

More huffing, more puffing and more eye-rolling...

Aleeta didn't know what to do at this point. This man was bothering her but she needed to wash her hands, so she did, then took a closer look at him. Did she know this guy? She'd seen him at another hotel. He was doing maintenance there too and had the audacity to talk to her. Like she'd ever date a maintenance guy...

She was the face of Mountain View Beauty. A celebrity. What would she look like talking to someone so beneath her?

She waved her hand beneath the automatic paper towel dispenser, ripped off a towel then dried her hands angrily before leaving.

Drake screwed the old bulb out, put the lampshade back on for safety purposes and then packed up his things. The bulb wasn't one they kept in storage. It would have to be ordered. He was heading to the front desk to tell Joelle the same thing when he saw Aleeta talking to her.

"There he is," Aleeta said, pointing at Drake as he approached the desk. "He needs to be fired!"

"You know for such a small frame you have a really big mouth," Drake told her.

"You're the one with the big mouth. A big disrespectful one. That's why you're stuck cleaning toilets—don't have any people skills."

"For your information, Mrs. Know It All, I don't clean toilets, but if I did, I'd need battery acid to clean the stall you came out of."

Joelle forced herself not to laugh. Well, she tried, but a snicker escaped. "Um...Dra— Drake," she said, trying to stop him from engaging in a back and forth with Aleeta.

He looked at her, saw the smirk on her face and smiled. He said, "I removed the bulb. I'll have to order it. It's not a..." he was still laughing. "It's not a normal stock item."

"Can you order it today?" Joelle asked.

"Sure can. I'll do it as soon as I get back to the office."

"Thank you, Drake."

"You're welcome. Let me get out of here so I'm not in the presence of *wannabe* royalty," he said looking at Aleeta.

"Blah, blah, *bleh*. Go clean some more toilets."

He was going to let it go and continue toward the exit but that inner voice that wanted to snap couldn't be quiet. He walked back to the counter and said, "Jo, you should do background checks on the people we let up in here. Some folks don't deserve to use our hotels."

Drake walked away before Aleeta could reply with a slick, eye-rolling comment.

Heated, Aleeta looked at Joelle said, "I asked around. Everybody suggested this place for the kind of event I'm planning."

"As they should," Joelle said trying to do damage control after she'd almost cracked a rib holding in laughter. "The lodge has ample space—"

"But rude workers," Aleeta darted out.

"Aleeta, I can assure you we employ top-notch professionals in all fields, from the maids on down to the employees in our restaurant."

"Then how do you explain the maintenance man?" she asked, then pursed her lips.

"Um…he's not our usual," Joelle told her. It was the truth.

"Well, he's rude and I don't like him. Need I remind you I know Remington Lennox personally."

And? Joelle hid a smirk. So what she knew

Remington? She wasn't family – just a rich, spoiled hussy who was accustomed to getting her way. Still, Joelle cleared her throat and pulled some customer service skills out of the bag and said, "Let me handle this for you, Aleeta. You have enough to worry about already. I'll make sure the rest of your stay goes smoothly. Anything you need, just let me know."

"Thank you. Now *that's* the kind of service I expect."

"Of course," Joelle said. She even made herself smile, all the while hoping Aleeta didn't come back to the desk for anything. Ever.

Aleeta put the earphones back in her ear and left the desk, strutting toward the banquet room where she was supposed to be meeting with her assistant to go over the Winter Wonderland theme for the new product launch. Everything needed to be perfect. There couldn't be any more distractions, especially not from an overbearing, obnoxious maintenance guy.

Chapter 2

Drake drove back to his office, peeled off the blue jumpsuit and fixed his clothes – getting back into work mode – his *normal* work. He was still ticked off about the stuck up broad running her mouth but he wouldn't allow it to ruin his day.

<<Ring. Ring.>>

His cell phone alerted his attention. He saw Joelle's number on the display. He'd expected a call from her, but he hadn't known it would come so soon.

He answered, "If you're calling about Aleeta..."

"Drake, what happened?"

Joelle asked the question in a way that he could tell she'd been laughing prior.

He asked, "What do you mean *what happened*?"

"You know what I mean. What happened? In the bathroom? With Aleeta?"

"Forget about it. It was nothing," he told her, trying to end it.

"Drake Lennox, if you don't start talking..."

"Look, I was just doing my job. I went into the bathroom to change the bulb. *Big Mouth* comes out one of the stalls screaming and staring at me like I'm an apparition."

Joelle laughed.

"I'm serious, Jojo. She had this weird look on her face like her life was in danger."

"Well, in her defense, it's not every day you find a man in the ladies' bathroom. I was trying to stop you when you were passing through the lobby. I knew she had just gone in there, but I couldn't get your attention."

"It doesn't matter now," Drake said kicking his feet up on the desk, crossing his legs at the ankles.

"It *does* matter. Like it or not Aleeta brings major business for Lennox Enterprises—not to mention she likes throwing Remy's name out every time she thinks something is not going her way."

"She knows Remy?"

"She does. They went to the same college but it wasn't like they were friends or anything. All I know is, I don't want no drama over here while I'm trying to work. And did you really tell the girl she looked like a pitbull puppy?"

Drake threw his head back and laughed. "I did."

"You're so mean." She laughed too.

"She had it coming. I gave her the same energy she was giving me, but no worries Jojo.

There won't be no more drama, especially from my end."

"Good. Have you ordered that bulb yet?"

"No. I just got here, girl. Can a brother breathe for five minutes?"

"A brother can give me an ETA on that bulb."

"You drive a hard bargain. Is this what Giovanni has to put up with?"

Joelle laughed. "You better hush before I get a woman on your butt to get your tail in check. Like Aleeta..."

"Nah, I'm good."

"That's what they all say. Anyway, the phones are going nuts. I gotta run. I'll be waiting for my bulb."

"Yes, Sarge."

She giggled. "Bye, Drake."

"Later, girl."

He placed his cell on the desk, turning his attention to a stack of resumes he'd printed out. He had five positions to fill. He was growing tired of running out to different sites to make repairs when it was no longer his job. Whether he liked it or not (and he didn't like anything about the interviewing process) he had to fill those empty positions with bodies unless he wanted to continue playing the role of on-call maintenance guy. That was a job he didn't want, especially if he had to run into people like Aleeta Cofield. On what planet did she think it was acceptable to assert herself as superior to anyone she met? Why did people who thought they'd made a name for themselves try to convince other people they were unimportant or less than? Her face was on a few billboards and Mountain View Beauty had over one million subscribers on YouTube and Instagram. So what? Did status dictate how people should be treated?

He couldn't fathom such an idiotic idea. If that were the case, he'd walk around with his nose to the ceiling, looking down on the workers beneath him – the ones that actually went out into the field and made things happened. But he didn't do that, nor would he ever. He knew what it was like to be one of them. It's where he'd come from. Even if he were a millionaire, which he wasn't, that wouldn't make him look down on anybody. People deserved to be treated with dignity and respect. That's a lesson Aleeta needed to learn.

Chapter 3

Drake chucked the football so far, it went beyond the marked end zone. It was intentional. Their family's traditional Saturday football game wouldn't go as planned as long as the crew kept on bringing up Aleeta's name. Whenever Drake threw the ball, the comment was: *Yeah throw it like Jojo threw you out of the lodge for embarrassing that Aleeta chick.*

When Drake caught the ball somebody said: *Look y'all. He caught the ball like he caught Aleeta Cofield copping a squat.*

"All right, all right. Time out," Drake said.

"It's too cold out here for timeouts, Drake," Kenton said.

Everyone had on hats, coats and gloves except for the men who were playing the game. They wore long sleeve shirts and hats since they were working up a sweat running back and forth across the slippery field. In forty-degree weather, they would only stay warm if they kept moving.

"Why are you calling timeout, man?" Remington asked.

"So y'all can get all of these sly *Aleeta* jokes out of your system. Go ahead. Let's hear 'em."

Remington raised his brows. "I'm trying to ball. I got nothing."

Kenton said, "I got something. How many Lennoxes does it take to change a light bulb?"

"How many?" Spencer asked.

"I don't know. Ask Drake," was his answer. He cracked up laughing, bending over with his hand on his knees.

"That ain't even funny," Drake said.

Spencer said, "Ay, be honest, Drake. Did you sneak a peek?"

"Nope," Drake answered.

"Why were you in there, anyway?" Giovanni asked. He blew breath into his hands, attempting to warm them temporarily.

"I was changing a light bulb. Don't pretend Jojo hasn't told you the whole story, Vanni."

Drake looked over at Joelle. She was propped up against her car, chatting with the other women in the Lennox family – Jessalyn, Spencer's wife. A pregnant Emory, Remington's wife. Lauren, Kenton's wife. And then there was Davina Lennox – the youngest of the Lennox siblings.

Drake said, "I think Jojo set me up."

Joelle smiled when she heard what he'd said. "I didn't set you up, Drake."

"Yeah, she didn't set you up," Giovanni said clutching the football with one hand, pretending to throw it. "Why are you blaming your insane behavior on my wife?"

"Because she just couldn't wait for one of my guys to change the bulb. Mrs. Efficient *had* to have her problem fixed then and there."

"That's how Jojo rolls," Kenton said.

"Yeah. She's married to me," Giovanni said. "My baby's accustomed to instant gratification with her pretty self." He bit down on his lips as he looked over at her.

"Then I hope she calls you to change the bulb the next time."

"Nope," Giovanni blurted out. "Not my area of expertise, man."

Remington chuckled. "How difficult could it be to change a light bulb?"

"Trust me—this ain't no ordinary bulb," Drake said. "Y'all went all fancy with the upgrades to the lodge. I had to special-order the replacement. You know it's a problem when you can't just pull up to a Lowe's or Home Depot and buy it."

Remington brushed grass and dirt off of his pants. "Are we playing football or having a team meeting out here?"

"Looks like a meeting, babe," Emory shouted as she placed a hand on her stomach. Remington looked over at her and winked. She was bundled up – wearing a white puffy coat, hat, and gloves – the whole nine. He had wanted her to stay home but she didn't want to miss an opportunity to hang out with the family no matter how frequently they saw each other.

"Look—the bottom line is, you need to get Aleeta in check, Rem," Drake said.

An amused look flashed across Remington's face. "*I* need to get her in check?"

"Yeah. She thinks she has clout because y'all went to college together or something."

"I don't know her like *that*, but hey, the bottom line is this is business. She's looking for a place to host her big winter product reveal and she, or her team or whoever, has chosen the lodge."

"So, why does everyone seem to walk on eggshells around this woman?" Kenton asked.

Giovanni frowned. "Everyone like who?"

"Well, Jojo for one."

"Jojo what?" Joelle asked. "Why are y'all talking about me?"

Giovanni came to his wife's defense saying, "Jojo ain't walking on eggshells. My wife's a perfectionist. She wants everything to run smoothly at the lodge."

"But that's not possible," Kenton said. "Everything doesn't run smoothly all the time."

"Either way it goes, the lodge is the top-grossing hotel at Lennox Enterprises."

"Yeah, yeah, yeah," Drake said. How many times had he heard that?

"Okay, so how do you think it got that way?" Giovanni asked, then followed up with, "I'll tell you. Got that way because Jojo's a hard worker. If she's going to bat for this Aleeta person, she sees value in it for our entire organization. We need to do whatever we can to support it."

"Took the words right out of my mouth," Remington said patting his younger brother on the shoulder. "This is why I made him the district manager."

Spencer jumped in to ask, "Isn't Aleeta Cofield the woman with the beauty products that costs two arms and four legs?"

"Yep. That's her," Drake responded.

"Jess ordered some face cream from them—two fluid ounces cost eighty bucks."

Remington nodded. "Sounds about right. Emory uses it, too."

"So, how are you going to proceed?" Spencer asked Drake. "This woman sounds like trouble. Is she worth it?"

"Absolutely," Remington answered. "Mountain View Beauty has a huge event every quarter and each one brings in at least $200,000 in revenue. My advice to Jojo was to give Aleeta what she wants but within reason. Let's stick with that plan for now. Agreed?"

"The CEO has spoken," Drake said. "I'm with it."

"Just stay out of the women's bathroom and everything should flow just fine," Kenton said.

"All right, enough talking," Remington said. "Let's get back into this game."

Giovanni chuckled, tossing Remington the football. "Why are you so anxious to get your butt whooped, bruh?"

"You'll be changing your tune soon enough," Remington said.

"That's right. Get him, babe," Emory said

cheering her husband on from the sidelines.

Drake smiled, distracted by their interaction. Emory was pregnant and Remington was beyond ecstatic. Lately, he'd been thinking if that could be his reality one day – falling in love with a beautiful woman, having a family. Sharing a home. Sharing life. Being happy. If Remington and Emory's relationship was any indicator of how sweet life could be, he was ready to start living that kind of life now. But he had to find his queen first.

Chapter 4

A Week Later

Drake had the bulb delivered to his office. It had been dropped off thirty minutes ago. He didn't call Joelle to notify her because he knew what her next question would be – when are you coming to install it? He took a proactive approach. He jumped in the truck and headed over to Smoky Mountain Lodge. He was dressed casually today – a navy blue polo sweater-vest with a white shirt underneath and a pair of jeans, but he also looked preppy like he belonged to one of those prestigious universities that celebrities paid millions of dollars for their less-than-average kids to get into.

"Good morning, sunshine," he said to Joelle upon entering the lobby.

"Hey you," Joelle responded. "You got the bulb, I see."

Drake held it up like a torch. "I do."

"You're still short guys this week?" Joelle asked, trailing him.

"I could've sent someone today."

"Then why didn't you?" she inquired.

"Because I started it and I told you I was going to finish it."

They stopped in front of the bathroom door. "Can you go inside and make sure your evil friend isn't in there flying around hittin' switches on her broom?"

Joelle snickered. "Keep your voice down. *And* she isn't my friend. She's a client of Lennox Enterprises. Remember that."

Drake lifted a brow. He wasn't with all that pleasing-the-client-by-any-means-necessary nonsense. Maybe he needed to work on his customer service skills. In the meantime, all he was focusing on was installing the bulb and getting out of dodge.

"Give me the all-clear so I can get out of here, Jojo."

Joelle went in, confirmed no one was inside then relayed the information to Drake. Then she stood watch outside while he went in and screwed and secured the bulb into place, along with the lampshade. He brushed his hands together after putting the tools back into the toolbox then picked it up and pulled the bathroom door open to exit. He looked to the left – looked to the right – there was no sign of Joelle.

And she was supposed to be keeping watch...

She wasn't at the front desk, either, he noticed. He was about to head out when he heard her say, "Hey, Drake, is it all fixed now?"

"Yeah. It's fixed. Weren't you supposed to be guarding the door?"

"I was, but then I had to go help somebody with something."

"Sounds like a second round of setups."

She giggled. "Drake, I never set you up. Stop it. Why would I do that to you?"

His eyes narrowed skeptically. "That's a good question."

"I wouldn't. Now, before you run off, I can use your help with something else."

"Jo, I know you think I am, but I'm not your personal assistant."

"I know. Just come here," she said taking him by the arm.

"Come where? Where are you taking me, girl?"

"To the banquet room."

"Is Satan back there?"

Joelle laughed. "Stop it, Drake."

"You're laughing which means you already know who I'm talking about so *you* stop it."

"My goodness. What am I going to do with you?"

She stepped into the ballroom.

Drake looked around. The place was bare except for the round tables that were pushed up against the walls, leaving a wide-open area probably so Aleeta could envision her plan for the launch party. There was one table that remained right side up – and there was a woman sitting there with curly her hair pulled back with a clip. It's the table where Joelle was taking him.

"Who's that?" Drake whispered.

"Hold on. I'll introduce you."

"Introduce me to who?" he whispered again, a little louder.

"Wait for the introduction, Drake."

When they were steps away from the table, Joelle said, "Hey, Lavina. I'm back with backup. This is my cousin Drake Lennox. Drake, this is Lavina Nelson."

Lavina stood up from the table and reached to shake Drake's hand. The moment her hand touched his, it quivered. And when she looked into his honey-colored eyes, she froze faster than a sheet of ice on an overpass. The man was fine. No, not fine. *Foine!* Had she ever seen a man so handsome? He had that stilling effect that made women's hearts palpitate. His hair was cut to a fade – dark black hair that offset the color of his incredible eyes. Eyes so gorgeous, they didn't look real. Lips so firm looking, she imagined what they might've felt like. Bone structure so on point, he looked like he special-ordered his face from his maker. The dark lashes, eyebrows, mustache and beard – Drake Lennox was solidly handsome.

Lavina was drooling in a sense. She didn't run up on men usually, especially one like him. Lavina shied away from men. If she wanted to experience the thrill and excitement of meeting a new guy, she'd do what she'd been doing – live vicariously through her best friend Aleeta.

Drake cleared his throat, glanced at Joelle as if to say (what have you gotten me into now?) then looked back at Lavina. She was still holding his hand looking at him like she was caught up in a dream – like he was the piece of cake and she was the fat kid.

And she still had his hand for some reason. He felt the way her hand quivered when she first connected it with his and he had no idea why she was nervous. Wasn't it like an everyday practice for strangers to shake hands and be cordial?

And who was this woman rocking a pair of red-rimmed glasses, looking like she was intimidated by him? She looked young – young but tired. Her hair was black and curly. Face, delicate. Eyes, brown. Skin, the color of melted milk chocolate. She had some dominant cheekbones like she'd had some Indian in her blood. Probably had. Most people did around this neck of the woods.

Joelle cleared her throat and said, "Drake is in charge of maintenance at our hotels and resorts."

"I am. Um, do you think I can have my hand back now?" Drake asked her.

"Oh. Sure. Yes. Sorry," she said, sounding panicky. "I zoned out for a moment there."

Drake grinned. "No worries. It happens to the best of 'em."

"Oh my gosh," Joelle mumbled, amused.

"I'm Lavina. Nelson. Lavina Nelson."

"Right," Drake said. Joelle had introduced her already, so he knew her name. "Nice to meet you, Lavina Nelson."

"You as well."

Joelle said, "Lavina is helping Aleeta organize the event for Saturday."

Okay...what does that have to do with me? He wasn't a part of any event planning committee so why was Joelle introducing him to Lavina?

"I have a question," Lavina said looking directly at him.

He tried not to frown. Tried, but failed. One came through. This pretty little petite woman was talking to the wrong person. He had to get back to the office. He had resumes to review. Interviews to schedule. People to hire. Positions to fill.

"Um, do you have a minute?" Lavina asked him.

"No, I don't, but since I'm already here, what—"

"Awesome. My theme for this banquet room is *Winter Wonder*," she said. "You know like *Wonderland* but without that *land*."

"Yeah...don't take a genius to figure that one out."

Joelle elbowed him.

"I thought that was cool, although my boss said it sounded stupid. Aleeta likes *Winter Wonderland* better. Anywho, I wanted to ask you if we could string lights across the ceiling. They'll be hanging lights on a string. Do you know what I mean?"

"Yeah. I—"

"String lights," Lavina interrupted Drake to say. "Lights on an...um...string."

"I got the concept of string lights. How many are you planning on having?"

"A whole wop of them."

"I'm sorry, did you say *wop*?"

Joelle giggled softly.

"Yes," Lavina answered.

"How much is a wop?"

"A bunch."

Drake squinted. Was he asking the wrong questions because he surely was getting the wrong answers? "Okay, well I would need to know the wattage to determine if your *wop* of lights would pose a fire risk. We've already had a fire at one of our resorts—don't want another one, Lavina. Nelson."

"Yes, Sir."

Drake's eyes narrowed. "Sir? Did you just call me *Sir*?"

"Yes, Sir. I mean, yes Mr. Lennox. Would you prefer Mr. Lennox instead?"

He smirked.

Joelle said, "I'll leave you two at it. I need to head back to the front desk."

Drake nor Lavina acknowledged what Joelle said. They were too engrossed with their weird conversation. Well, weird for him – normal for her.

"You don't have to call me Sir," Drake told her. "How old are you?"

"I'm twenty-six," Lavina said, "And calling you *Sir* has nothing to do with age for me. It's more about respect."

Drake appreciated that but, at the same time, he didn't want to be treated like an old man either. He said, "I'm okay with *Drake*."

"Are you sure?"

"It's my name. Yes, I'm sure." Drake rotated his wrist to check the time. It was close to lunch and since the Smoky Mountain Lodge had a restaurant attached, he thought it would be convenient to eat here before returning to his office. He looked at Lavina and asked, "Ay, why don't we discuss these *lights* over lunch."

"Lunch?" she said. Sounded like a question...

He hid a smile. "Yes. Lunch. You know...food. Eat. Yum-yum. Stomach grumbling then stomach not grumbling anymore."

"Of course," she said tickled. "I was just curious why you're asking me and not Aleeta."

Aleeta? What was this girl talking about? "Aleeta isn't here is she? You are. I'm asking you."

"Okay," Lavina said, "But I don't have a lot of time. Aleeta wants what she wants and when something isn't done right she'll go nuts and fly off the handle."

"You mean the broom handle?"

Lavina giggled. "So, you've met her."

"Oh, I've had my run-in with her and don't want another."

He gestured for her to proceed ahead of him as they walked into the restaurant. They quickly ordered food and was in the beginning *quiet* stage of chowing down when he asked, "How long have you worked for Mountain View Beauty?"

"Since the company's inception. The products are my recipes."

"Really?" he asked. This was news to him. From everything he knew about the company, Aleeta was the mastermind behind it and the brand.

"Yes."

"All of them?" he questioned.

"Yep."

"Then for everything related to Mountain View Beauty, why's Aleeta's face plastered on all the billboards around here?"

Lavina grabbed a napkin and wiped her mouth before she said, "She's a part of the company and my best friend."

"Come again?"

"She's my best friend. We grew up together. Went to college together."

"Then you know Remington Lennox. My cousin."

"I know of him. Yes. I don't know him-*know him* if you know what I mean."

"I do. Tell me more about the company."

"More like what?"

"How did it come about?"

"It started from an assignment in college. I came up with a skincare regimen in a business class. Our assignment was to make a product from scratch and since I've always had problematic skin, I researched ingredients to make a natural, chemical-free product that could help clear acne."

"It worked," Drake said staring at her. "Your skin is beautiful."

She blushed. Did he really think her skin was beautiful or was he just making conversation? "Thanks."

"Welcome," he said. He took a sip of tea and didn't take his eyes off of her.

He wasn't trying to gas her up, but she had some amazing skin. Flawless and glowing. From the looks of it, her hair was pretty, too, but he couldn't see it in all its glory since she had it clipped back. Made him wonder why her pretty brown face wasn't on any of the billboards for her own products.

She pushed her glasses on her face more securely. "So, anyway, I pitched the skin cream to my professor and he loved it. He told me as long as I have some good marketing and product presentation, it would be a hit. I didn't have any kind of startup money for the business but Aleeta's parents were well off. So, she gave me some money with the promise I'd pay them back and give her a role in the company, so that's what I did. I make the products and she convinces people they need the products."

"Has she developed anything of her own?"

"No. I do the developing. I'm the owner and product development manager."

Owner? If she was the owner, why did she refer to Aleeta as the boss?

"So, what's the product development manager doing hanging around this dump?"

Lavina laughed – more like snorted. Embarrassed, she covered her mouth and then took a sip of tea. "If Joelle heard you say that..."

"She knows I'm only teasing. This place is a five-star, top-of-the-line property. Rooms go for two-hundred a night and it stays booked year-round. I see why your boss picked this place. Wait—if Mountain View Beauty is your company, why do you call Aleeta your boss again?"

"She's the face of the company and being such, she's kinda taken on the leadership role. Pretty much what she says goes."

He saw no logic in her answer, but it wasn't his place to speak on how other people ran their business – especially folks he didn't know.

"But enough about all that. Let's talk about lights," Lavina said.

"Right, because Lavina Nelson has a thing for lights."

Her cheeks went crimson for a second time. "Me and Aleeta came up with this winter-themed party together, but the lights—those are *my* idea."

"You're proud of that, aren't you?"

"I am."

"Have you looked into battery-operated lights? I've seen people use those for weddings and whatnot," he said. Instantly his eyes went to her left hand – ring finger. It was vacant.

"I have. The problem with that is, I can't find

the ones I want in the battery version."

"But you found them in electric form?"

"Yes."

"What about a comparable battery-version?"

She shook her head. "I want the ones I found."

"Looks like Aleeta isn't the only one who *wants what she wants.*"

Lavina smiled. "Looks that way, but I've been after these lights for some time. I already have them loaded into my cart online but haven't submitted the order yet."

Drake wiped his mouth and hands then took out his cell phone. "What's your number?"

"My—my number like my cell phone number or the business number for Mountain View Beauty?"

Drake looked at the woman sideways. Was she serious? He said, "I want the number where if I were to dial it right now, I'd hear something ring or vibrate on your side of the table."

"Cell phone number it is then," she said then rattled off her phone number.

He keyed it in, dialed it and heard the moment her phone rang. "Save my number in your phone. When you get a chance, look into your online cart, pull the specs on those lights and screenshot them to me."

"Will do."

He watched her eat for a moment. She'd told him she was twenty-six but she looked younger. A *lot* younger. The lenses of the glasses made her eyes appear bigger. She looked plain and unmade and something was exquisitely beautiful and innocent about that. But it was also that *something* that was holding her back. He got the feeling she didn't want to accentuate her beauty. She was okay with being hidden – letting her friend, Aleeta, have the spotlight and Aleeta was all-too happy to take it.

"Welp, it's been real Lavina, but I have to get back to the office." Drake stood up. "I'll be waiting for your call."

She cringed. "Call? I thought you said text?"

He took out his wallet and left a fifty on the table. "Call, text, telegraph—whatever you're comfortable with."

"Okay. Thanks again."

"No problem."

"And thanks for lunch."

He stopped, turned around. Looked at her. "You're welcome."

Drake walked to the lobby and waved at Joelle.

"Hey, I thought you'd left already," Joelle said.

"I was in the restaurant...had to go grab some lunch with ol' girl."

"Who?"

"Lavina Nelson. She can't get enough of talking about those lights. I told her to send me the specs."

"Cool. Way to go the extra mile to satisfy our customers, Drake."

"Yeah, whatever. Let me get out of here

before you assign me something else." He did a double drum tap on the desk and said, "I'm out."

"Bye, Drake."

"See ya, and don't call me no more today. If I see your name flash across my phone, I'm sending you to voicemail."

"Whatever," she said laughing.

Chapter 5

Drake spent the morning interviewing. The *entire* morning. Throughout each one, he'd check his phone periodically to see if Lavina had called or texted him about the lights, but she hadn't. He couldn't say he was surprised. She'd probably forgotten all about the lights with the many other responsibilities of planning the product launch event scheduled for Saturday. But since today was Tuesday, she needed to order the lights ASAP to ensure their arrival at least by Thursday evening – Friday morning at the latest.

That's why after his last interview, he hopped in the truck and drove to the hotel. He had Lavina's number – he could've called, but he didn't want to.

Joelle was surprised to see Drake today. She hadn't called him for anything, so why was he there exactly? She said, "You're on a roll, aren't you? What are you doing here?"

"Got some unfinished business to take care of."

"And you had to get dressed up to do it huh, GQ?" she asked checking out the black suit he had on. And did he have a fresh cut and lineup? And what was that deliciousness tickling her nose? Cologne?

"I've been interviewing all morning—have to look the part."

"Well, in the words of Madea, hallelujah, praise the *lort*!" she exclaimed. "You nailed it. And lemme tell you something else—the *lort* knows you need to hire every person who walked through your door this morning."

Drake laughed.

So did she. "So, what unfinished business do you have to take care of in my precious kingdom?"

He glanced to the right and saw the *unfinished business* in question. She had those glasses on again, pushed on tight to her face heading straight for them. Drake attempted to break the stare, but he couldn't turn away. Something about her spoke to him. Was it those jeans – ones that clung to her impressively curvy body shape? Didn't look like she had any more room in them like that woman Ginuwine was singing about. She was slim but thick in all the right places. Slim-thick. Yeah, that's what she was. The big white sweater she wore drowned out the top half of her body. And her hair was the same as when he saw her yesterday – clipped back. He could only imagine how it would look draped around her sweet, chocolate face.

"Um...Drake...?" Joelle said, trying to get his attention, but he didn't hear her. Lavina had his attention. All of it.

And Drake had Lavina's attention – all of it. Her, and them jeans.

"Good morning, Lavina Nelson," he said to her when she was only a few steps away.

"Good morning, Sir. I mean, Drake." Her eyes narrowed. "It is *Drake*, right?" She stammered pushing those glasses on her face again. Drake was convinced that if she pushed them any further, they'd become a permanent part of her skull.

"Yes, it's Drake, and you owe me something, girl."

She looked confused for a moment as she tried to figure out what she owed him. Then she said, "Oh. Duh. The specs. I forgot all about it."

"Yeah, sure you did..." he said staring at her lips. Full lips. How had he not noticed them yesterday? The moment she smiled, his heart skipped a beat. When had his heart ever done a foolish thing like that? The girl was giving him atrial fibrillation.

"You don't believe me?" she asked.

"Nope."

She laughed nervously. "I honestly forgot," she admitted, staring up into those whiskey-colored eyes of his, getting drunk in them. What was he doing so dressed up today? Rocking a black suit, he looked like he had all the swag in the world. And he smelled good, too. She'd never smelled that brand of cologne before, but it was so far embedded up her nostrils, whenever she smelled it from this point forward, she'd think of him. Drake Make-A-Woman-Blush Lennox.

"When can you get that information to me, Lavina Nelson?" he asked taking a step closer to her.

Lavina took a step back.

He took another step forward.

She took another back.

He took another forward. If she wanted to *dance*, he'd dance.

She raised her brows.

He flashed a devilish grin.

She chewed on her bottom lip.

His eyes feasted on that lip...

Joelle watched all of this go down.

"What information do you need?" Drake heard someone ask from behind him.

He turned around and there stood Aleeta to his dissatisfaction. For someone with such a pretty face, she had a nasty attitude.

He asked, "Hey, where's your broom?"

She frowned. Her nose went up like an unpleasant order had found its way to her nostrils. "Broom? Oh, I see...the *maintenance man* is trying to be funny today since he showered and put on a suit."

"This is what I usually wear to work," Drake told her. "As the head of maintenance for Lennox Enterprises, I have to look the part and set a good example for those who work under me. You should try doing the same for the people who break their necks every day that cater to you." He hadn't intended on telling her what his real job was, but in the words of Jay-Z, sometimes you needed your ego to remind these fools...

She flipped her weave and said, "Oh boo-who-freakin'-who...is this person bothering you, Lavina?"

"No, he—"

"Lavina's a grown woman," he interrupted her to say. "She doesn't need you coming to her rescue."

"Um, guys...I'm right here," Lavina drawled, raising her hand.

They both looked at her. So did Joelle but her attention went to the phone shortly thereafter.

"I have work to do," Aleeta said then stomped off in a pair of Louboutin's that she hadn't quite mastered walking in. Those poor red-bottoms were doing the *lean wit' it, rock wit' it*.

Drake was left shaking his head as she walked away.

Joelle hung up the phone.

Drake said, "You know what? I'll be right back." He headed in the same direction Aleeta had wobbled off in.

Lavina flashed a look of defeat when she turned to Joelle and said, "That's amazing how Aleeta does that."

"Does what?"

"Be all rude and neck-snappy, yet still manage to put men under her spell. I wish I had that ability."

Joelle lifted a brow. "Wait—you think Drake is under this so-called *spell*?"

"Obviously," she said gesturing toward him as he continued to the banquet room.

Joelle looked that way. What exactly was Drake doing? She could've sworn he was feeling Lavina so why had he excused himself to go talk to Aleeta?

"I don't think men are necessarily bothered by rudeness. Men like what appeals to their eyes. They'll tolerate a woman with a bad attitude and pretty face until they grow weary of the attitude."

"Meanwhile, us good girls get overlooked."

Joelle flashed a weak smile. Even though Lavina hadn't said outright who she was talking about, Joelle knew this was all Drake-related.

"Well, look on the bright side. You're young. And smart. And beautiful. Somebody will come along who appreciates that. In fact, I have an idea. Why don't you come to the fire pit tonight? Every Tuesday night, the hotel gives out s'more packets so guests can make s'more around the fire and get to know each other."

"Isn't the temperature supposed to be on Antarctica tonight?"

"Yes, but it won't feel like it around an open fire."

"Uh...hmm...I don't know." Lavina thought about it and said, "I may be there. Are you going?"

"Only for a few minutes to drop off the goodies, but me and *fire* have a bad history so I can't stay too long."

"Okay."

* * *

Drake walked into the banquet room behind Aleeta. He said, "And another thing—I've been doing some research on your *company* and imagine my surprise to find out you're not the owner nor the manager of Mountain View Beauty."

"What business is that of yours?"

"What business is it of yours to insult my profession when, if it wasn't for Lavina's brilliance and business know-how, you wouldn't have one."

"Oh, and I suppose you feel like you worked your way to the top and wasn't just handed your job because *Lennox* is your last name."

"No one has ever handed me anything. I worked hard for everything I have. You, on the other hand, are a taker. You represent yourself as the founder and CEO of this company to the point where you have the company's true owner, Lavina, calling you *boss*."

"Yeah, that's right. I *am* the boss and she knows it. Do you really think Lavina could handle the amount of pressure I deal with on a daily basis with this company? I'll answer that for you. No! She's too soft-spoken. She's smart, I'll give her that, but she doesn't have what it takes to be in the spotlight. She just doesn't have it. Come on. You've seen her."

"Wow!" Drake said. "How can you call yourself a *friend*—her *best* friend—after saying something like that?"

Aleeta shrugged and folded her laptop open. "Lavina knows the dynamics of our friendship and business relationship. You're an outsider. You don't get it."

"Oh, I get it. I just hope one day she does."

Drake couldn't leave the room fast enough. Aleeta was a leech as far as he was concerned, and she didn't mind taking advantage of Lavina since she knew how shy she was. Aleeta was in no way a friend to Lavina, and Lavina was walking around like Sandra Bullock in *Birdbox*.

He walked back to the check-in desk. Joelle had just hung up the phone.

"Hey, where'd Lavina go?" he asked, sliding his hands into the pockets of his slacks.

"Not sure. Why are you looking for her now, anyway?" she asked, crossing her arms. "I thought you were busy chasing *Aleeta*."

"You thought—" He frowned. "You thought I was interested in that psycho broad?"

"Yeah."

He erupted in laughter. "You of all people should know better than that, Jojo."

"Right, but when you ditched Lavina to go talk to Aleeta, I didn't know what to think."

"I didn't ditch Lavina. Listen to me very closely, Jo—I'd rather be mauled by a couple of bears than be seen with that Aleeta chick."

"Then why'd you chase her?"

"I didn't chase her. I went to confront her."

"About what?"

"She—" he started, then hesitated. He was supposed to be avoiding drama. "Nothing."

"If this has something to do with the hotel, Drake—"

"Settle down, Jojo. It's nothing." He sighed, took his right hand from his pocket and checked his watch. "I hate that I missed Lavina."

"She hates that she missed you, too."

"Did she say something?"

"Not directly, but I'm a woman. I can read between the lines, unlike y'all menfolk."

"So, what's between the lines?"

"That she likes you, dude!"

He smirked. He already knew that. He liked her, too. "Hey, do me a favor and call me when she gets back."

"Okay," she said amidst the ringing phone. "By the way, I told her about the campfire. She'll probably be there tonight."

"How do you know?"

"Just a hunch."

"Ah'ight. I'll be back later, then."

Chapter 6

Strangers sitting around toasting marshmallows...

Lavina smiled awkwardly at the guests and avoided eye contact with everyone. Why had she let Joelle talk her into doing this? It was freezing outside. The temperature had dropped to thirty-something. It was so cold, even the fire had a sho-hate-it moment and had to be restarted. But Lavina came prepared. She had gloves, a hat, a thick coat and a pair of boots.

"It's going to be a challenge making a marshmallow sammich with those wool gloves on, girl?" Drake said, sitting on a bench next to her.

"A what?" she asked tickled.

"You heard me. A marshmallow sammich. What'd you do? Grab a pair of clippers and jump a herd of sheep before you got here?"

Lavina laughed. "My mother bought me these gloves," she said stretching her hand out in front of her.

"I'm teasing. They look like they're keeping your hands nice and warm, unlike my hands."

"You need to get a little closer to the fire," she told him.

"Definitely."

She took what looked like a kabob stick and secured two marshmallows on the end of it. Drake did the same then held it near the fire pit.

"So, what does a guy gotta do to get specs on some string lights?"

She slapped herself on the forehead. "I forgot again!"

"Your memory is as bad as a politician's under oath."

After she stopped laughing, she said, "That's what happens when you have a lot on your plate. Hold on." Lavina pulled off her right glove then dug her cell phone from her coat pocket. She pulled up the online cart, clicked on the lights and took a screenshot of the specifications. After pulling up her text-messaging app, she attached the image and sent it to Drake. "There. Now you have it."

"Yeah, ten years later..." he said glancing at her, watching those pretty lips of hers form into a smile. Screw the cold – that alone was enough to warm his entire body.

The fire crackled, sending smoke and tiny sparkles of fire into the air. There was something deeply satisfying about the smell of burning firewood in an outdoor setting like this. It was like being in the comfort of his home, in front of the fireplace – well minus the thirty degrees and strangers all huddled around, playing the look-look away game.

Drake rubbed his hands together.

She said, "Would you like to use my gloves?"

He thought her offer was strange but sweet and selfless nonetheless. "Do I want to use your gloves?" He stretched out his hands and was already chuckling when he asked, "Do you think these hands will fit into those kid-sized gloves?"

She smiled. "*Kid size*...my hands aren't *that* small."

"They're much smaller than mine, sweetheart, but thank you. My hands are fine. If I get cold, I'll stand near the fire. Maybe I'll even jump in it—you know—to thaw out a bit."

She laughed softly while staring at the flames.

"Are you from the mountains?" he asked her.

"I am. My parents are still here."

"Where exactly is *here*?"

"Here. Cherokee."

"So, why are you staying at this hotel if you live in town?"

"For convenience. My room is full of stuff I need for the banquet. It's easier to carry items downstairs than haul it all in my car on the day of."

"Makes sense."

"What about you? Are you from here?"

"I'm from Bryson City."

"Oh...right around the corner."

"Yep. Right around the corner." He glanced over at her again. Seemed the glow from the fire worked wonders with her skin tone. He had wanted to pull those glasses off of her face to see the *real* her, but she probably wouldn't be able to see. The glasses looked serious.

Lavina could feel his eyes on her like she could feel the heat from the fire. She turned to look at him, then quickly looked away when her eyes burned into his intoxicating amber ones, focusing on roasting the marshmallows instead.

He smiled at the way they vibed off of each other.

She broke into their period of silence and said, "After I finished college I had dreams of moving to a big city like New York or Chicago and launching Mountain View Beauty there."

"Let me guess—Aleeta wanted to stay here. Look, just because her name implies that she's *a leader* doesn't mean Aleeta's a leader."

Lavina giggled. "Well, she made a good argument for staying. She said our products would change the community."

"You mean *your* products."

She smiled somewhat sadly and contemplative. "Yeah. She said she'd rather bring revenue here than to some big town where nobody knew who we were. Here, we're big fish in a small pond. There we would've been goldfish in an ocean."

"You're on fire," he said.

"I know," she said appreciatively. "The business is doing very well."

"No, I mean your marshmallows, baby girl. They're literally on fire."

"Oh shoot!" She waved the stick frantically to put out the blaze.

"He, you might want to..."

Before he could stop her from flailing the thing around, the smoke-crusted marshmallows flew off the stick and landed on the cement near the fire pit.

"Welp," Drake said tickled. "Those marshmallows are toast! Bye, marshmallows. It was nice to know y'all for the two minutes you were alive."

Lavina was slightly embarrassed, but she couldn't help but laugh.

"Why'd you cremate those marshmallows, girl?"

Lavina was laughing so hard now, tears came to her eyes. A few of the other guests who saw what happened we're laughing, too.

"You're funny," she told him. "I'm actually surprised you do this kind of thing."

"What thing?"

"This—sitting around a fire, toasting marshmallows."

"I usually don't do things like this."

"Ah...you must've thought Aleeta would be here."

"Hunh?" he asked. *Why would she say that?* "I wasn't—"

"She's somewhere pinching extra fat on her body trying to figure out a surgery that can remove it," Lavina said. "She's always striving to be a perfectionist—perfect body. Teeth. Hair. Everything."

"That's too bad. Nobody's perfect."

"Yeah, try telling her that."

"Here's the question of the century—why are you friends with her?" Drake asked.

Lavina shrugged. "It just happened that way, I guess. Her folks moved here when we were in the third grade. We've been best friends ever since."

"I've learned over the years that some relationships and friendships can do more harm than good."

She looked at him as he successfully made a s'more. A perfect one.

He continued, "I believe we keep some people in our lives because they're comfortable even though they're not necessarily *good* for us in the way of adding real value."

"Are you saying Aleeta isn't good for me?"

"I'm saying *some* people are not good for us. Here," he said handing her his s'more sandwich.

"No. I can't take yours."

"I insist," he said.

"Are you sure?"

"Very much so. Besides, your marshmallows look like Kingsford charcoal briquettes."

She smiled. "Stop picking on me. I've never done this before."

"Me either, but I've managed to make a perfect s'more and I want you to have it. Here. Take it. I don't want it. I happen to think marshmallows, chocolate and graham crackers are absolutely disgusting combination so have at it."

Lavina took a bite. And another. And another. "I don't know what you're talking about. This is good."

"I'll take your word for it."

"Again—if you don't like s'mores, why are you out here?"

He used his thumb to swipe a piece of marshmallow from the corner of her mouth.

"Thanks," she said.

"You're welcome, and to answer your question, I came out here because I was hoping to run into you," he said.

"Oh, yes...for the light specs."

Could she really be that oblivious to think he was only out here for information on the lights?

"I should have brought some water, milk or something out here."

"I'll get you some," Drake said. "Which would you prefer? Water or milk?"

"I'll take some milk."

Drake stood and said, "Be right back," then walked toward the side door entrance of the hotel. Lavina watched him walk away. The man wore a pair of jeans like good rappers rode beats. His walk was so natural and effortless. Drake Lennox wasn't who you'd picture as a maintenance guy. Well, he technically wasn't a maintenance guy any longer. He was an executive in a million-dollar organization. Aleeta had tried to portray his job as something to be looked down upon but there was a certain level of expertise and skill associated with fixing things when they malfunctioned. She had the utmost respect for the man she'd been getting to know for the last couple of days.

Lavina watched as Drake walked toward her with a sixteen-ounce container of white milk. She couldn't take her eyes off of him. He had on a brown leather jacket with his outfit and Timberland boots. He wasn't wearing a hat, although he probably should've been. He was the most handsome man that had ever given her any kind of *real* attention (what gives?!) and she didn't know what to do with it or him. At some point, she'd probably freeze up – intimidated by his brawny body and smooth brown skin. His complexion was a shade lighter than hers. And he had some big hands – big Paul Bunyan hands that looked like they could repair anything. Big strong hands. She could imagine those hands giving her a massage.

What are you thinking, Lavina? Why would he be interested in you? You're not Aleeta. Nothing like her. You're you and plain. And...you.

"Here you are, my dear," he said handing her the bottle.

"Thanks. That's so sweet of you."

"You're welcome. I couldn't sit around and let you choke off of those dry graham crackers."

Lavina opened the bottle. She took a long

drink, nearly downing half of it, then screwed the top back on. "Ahh," she said afterward, her thirst fully quenched. She could see her warm breath clashing with the cold air.

"Do you have siblings, Lavina?"

"I do. There are five of us—three girls and two boys—but they don't live here. My brothers live in New York. One sister is in Atlanta and the other lives in Greenville, South Carolina. I'm the only one who stayed home."

"I could be wrong but it sounds to me like you regret that."

"Sometimes I do. Here, I feel like I'm stuck in the monotony of life. Of the way things have always been."

"You have the company."

"Yeah, I have the company—one that I let Aleeta take over. Half the time, it doesn't feel like it's mine anymore."

"That's why you have to assert yourself as more of a boss than a silent partner. You're taking the lead on this new product launch for Saturday, right?"

"I am."

"Then make it the best launch party ever."

"Look at you being a coach. I like it."

"I'm serious, Lavina. I'm sure you invest a lot of time and energy into the recipes for your products."

"I do."

"So, you're passionate about it.

"I am."

"Then my advice to you is don't let the business side of the process ruin your passion.

There are a lot of people in the world who don't get the opportunity to see their passion to fruition and in case you're wondering, I'm not talking about myself. I never had a passion."

"No?" she asked. "I thought everybody kept something in their back pocket."

"I didn't have those dreams. I only wanted stable employment. That was my dream."

"And you found that, and as a bonus, you get to work with family."

"Yeah—those knuckleheads..."

She smiled. Drake looked at her. Her smile was beautiful. Everything about her was. She just kept it hidden.

"Well, it's been real," Lavina said standing, brushing graham cracker crumbs from her coat. "I have to be getting back to my room."

"Oh. I see what it is." Drake stood next to her. "You eat my food, chug down my milk and haul tail."

"I don't mean to run off, but I have a busy day tomorrow."

"Then I'll walk you to your room."

"Okay."

He walked in stride with her, then took a few quick steps to reach the door before she did. He pulled the handle and gestured for her to enter. They continued on to the elevator.

"What floor are you on?"

"Two."

"Ah...that's too bad...thought we'd have a longer ride."

A small smile touched her lips.

Drake pressed the button for the second floor, then looked at her.

She looked like she'd crawled back into a shell, standing as still as a statue. Out of nowhere, she said, "You're a funny guy."

"I am?" he asked, brows raised. He had good mind to take a step closer to her – hold her hostage in the corner, but he already knew she couldn't handle that. "Why am I funny?"

"The comment you made just now about a longer elevator ride."

The elevator doors dinged open. Drake gestured for her to exit first. "Is it so farfetched that I'd want to spend more time with you?"

"Um...yeah. It would be different," she told him as they walked toward her room.

"Why?"

She stopped in front of her door and pushed her glasses on her face more securely. "Because."

"*Because* isn't an answer. In fact, *because* stopped being an answer upon graduating from high school."

Her smile blossomed. "Okay, then. It would be different because men don't usually give me the time of day."

"That's because you haven't rolled up on the *right* man."

"You think that's what it is?" she asked staring into his eyes.

Drake's eyes danced from her eyes to her mouth. "I *know* that's what it is." He extended a hand to her.

She extended her gloved hand to him,

sealing the handshake.

He said, "I had a good time hanging out with you tonight."

"Yeah. It was nice."

Still holding her hand, he said, "I'll let you know about those lights tomorrow."

"Okay."

He released her hand – didn't want to – but he did. "Goodnight, Lavina."

"Goodnight, Drake."

He walked away from the door heading back for the elevator. She swiped her keycard, but before she stepped into the room, she stood there, watching him walk. And the man had a walk – one of those swagalicious ones that made women drool. He must've felt her eyes on him because he turned around. Lavina jumped, realizing she'd been caught. She pushed the door open and retreated inside of her room – heart pounding as she rested against the door.

"Shrew! Wow!"

She liked him. A lot. What would be the odds that he liked her the same? Is that how relationships worked? People *liked* each other like they were Facebook posts?

Why am I thinking about relationships? Especially with Drake? He's here to help me with the lights. Nothing more. Nothing less. Right?

"Right," she said aloud, answering her own question. But it was nice for a moment – to have some attention from a man, an attractive one – without being overshadowed by Aleeta, even if it was temporary.

Chapter 7

Drake found himself, yet again, at the lodge. He was so frequent now Joelle stopped asking him why he was there. She knew why and it all stemmed from the woman in the red-rimmed glasses.

Walking to the banquet room, he saw Lavina's rear end poking out from beneath a white tablecloth when he stepped into the room. What was she doing under the table?

He walked quietly across the carpet until he was standing directly behind her. When she moved to back up and move from under the table he shouted, "Boo!"

Startled, her whole body jerked. She inadvertently banged her head on the table.

"Ouch!" she said, holding her head as she emerged.

"Oh. Jeez. I didn't think I'd scare you *that* bad."

She was still holding her head, but the sting

she felt there had disappeared the moment her eyes landed on him.

He said, "Sorry about that, sweetie. Let me see if there's any damage."

He reached for her hair clip. Removed it.

She quickly gathered her hair in her fist. "No, it's fine, Drake."

"I got it," he said, removing her hand and releasing her hair. Her hair fell around her face. *All this pretty hair and you keep it hidden*, he thought to himself as he lost his hands in an ocean of curls. And it smelled good – smelled so good, he inhaled breaths of it.

"Where did you bump it?"

"Here," she said, pointing to the right, front side of her head.

"I got you," he told her, rubbing and massaging her there with his strong hands and muscular fingers.

Lavina could just die a pleasurable death here and now. How could someone contain so much energy and strength in their hands? Their fingers? Whatever pain she was feeling had long dissipated. This was heaven on earth. She had to fight to keep herself from moaning.

I should've bumped my head a long time ago...

"Is that better?" he asked.

"So much better," she replied.

"Umph, what's going on here?" Aleeta asked, sounding like a hater as she stepped into the banquet room.

Drake didn't acknowledge her. He should've known she was somewhere slithering around.

"Nothing," Lavina answered, quickly gathering her hair and securing it with the clip. "I bumped my head and Drake came to my rescue."

"Sure he did..." Aleeta mumbled then pretended to be busy but kept her eyes on Drake and Lavina.

Drake said, "You're good to go with those lights you wanted."

"Seriously?"

"Yes. I would recommend you order them today and pay extra for overnight shipping to guarantee they'll be here in time. I can help you hang them when they arrive."

"Okay, let me place this order right now before I forget." She pulled up the order on her phone. "Boom! It's done!"

"Good. Well, that's taken care of."

"Yep."

Aleeta took her laptop and left the room.

Drake looked at Lavina and said, "You didn't tell me Cruella De Vil would be here."

Lavina laughed. "Stop talking about my friend. She has her ways, but she's a good person."

"If you say so."

"Why don't you get along with her, anyway?"

"Why do you think I don't get along with her?"

"Because every time she's around, you have this constant frown on your forehead. Did she do something to you?"

"Yeah, she's rude. I came here to fix

something in the women's bathroom about a week and a half ago. Aleeta was in the bathroom even though she didn't reveal herself after I knocked and asked if anyone was inside. So I proceeded to set up shop. I had my tools on the floor and was removing a lampshade when *Cruella* comes out of a stall wearing earbuds. She screamed so loud, you would've thought she'd walked up on an ax murderer or something."

Lavina laughed. "That's about how I screamed when you scared me just now. You have a knack for scaring women, huh?"

"Nah. I scared you intentionally. Didn't know I would cause you to put a dent in your dome."

"I didn't bump my head *that* hard."

"Well, either way I need to make it up to you. So tell me—what can I do to assist you this morning, Lavina Nelson?"

"Um...I have to arrange these tables in a way that would give a center stage effect. We're having the stage set up on Friday. It's going to be in the middle of the room."

Drake looked around. "No problem, but I only have one caveat."

"What's that?"

"We have to be done by noon so we can have lunch together. I have to be back to my office for a meeting by 1:30."

She cracked a smile. Did he really slide lunch into her schedule for the day and work himself into it in the process? He did, and she didn't mind it one bit.

"Okay then. Let's get to work."

Chapter 8

They kept lunch simple – cheeseburgers and fries – and even in simplicity, they enjoyed what was a gourmet meal. The burgers at the lodge were to die for – so much so that people who weren't staying there would come to the restaurant specifically for them.

Drake had just taken another bite of his sandwich when he spotted Aleeta sitting at a corner table. Why did she always seem to pop up everywhere they were? "Your friend is here."

Lavina followed his eyes straight to Aleeta.

Aleeta flashed a pretentious smile – one that Drake could see was fake. She had a laptop in front of her and was eating some kind of a wrap.

"She's working on editing her latest YouTube video for our online campaign," Lavina said.

"Our?" Drake questioned. "How many videos have you done, Lavina?"

"None. I'm not really a person who likes the

spotlight."

"Maybe you should be."

"Huh?"

Drake wiped his hands. "The way I see it is, sometimes we can block your own blessings by not doing what we *know* we're supposed to be doing because of fear. Don't let fear keep you in second place when you're destined for first."

"How do you know what I'm destined for?"

"Because you created this company. You made something great and yet, you seem to run from it. Stop running from it. I think you should go to this launch and speak your mind. Let people know who you are. Oh, and by the way, I know a guy who'd love to be your date."

She blushed. "Do you now?"

"I do, and he's pretty fly—been sweatin' you all week. I think you'd like him."

"Wow. I'm—I'm flattered, Drake, but you know you don't have to right?"

"I want to," he said reaching across the table. He laid his hand on top of hers.

She glanced up at him then at his hand. Her hand twitched beneath his. "Thanks, Drake."

He gave a single nod then pulled his hand back and took a sip of Pepsi. "What are you wearing? We should color coordinate?"

"I don't have a gown yet."

"How could you *not* have a gown? The party is on Saturday."

"I know. I'm purposely procrastinating. I feel so uncomfortable in gowns. They always look frumpy on me."

With a body like hers, he seriously doubted that.

"Correct me if I'm wrong but don't you ladies typically try on gowns before you buy them?"

"Yes, but I usually just let Aleeta find something for me at the last minute."

Drake rubbed his hand across his mustache. *Aleeta strikes again.* Of course Aleeta would choose a gown that was less flattering for Lavina. It was all a part of her scheme to keep Lavina a silent partner so she didn't have to share the spotlight with anyone.

Not on his watch...

He said, "Joelle likes shopping and she knows where all the good *lady* stores are."

"*Lady* stores?" Lavina grinned.

"Yes. She'd love to take you around to try on some dresses."

"But Joelle's so busy running this place—"

"Trust me, she wouldn't mind. I'll set it up for you."

"No, that's okay, Drake. I don't want to be a nuisance."

"It won't be a problem. I can't let Aleeta choose a dress for you. You deserve to look like a princess at this party. *Your* party."

"I suppose it would be nice to choose my own gown for a change. I was imagining something frost blue."

"I think that will look lovely on you."

"And maybe I could ditch the glasses for contacts just for Saturday."

"Wait—you have contacts and you prefer to

wear glasses?"

"Well, I was never comfortable wearing contacts and Aleeta says the glasses give me an edge."

Aleeta.

Again.

Steering Lavina in the wrong direction...

While he thought she looked fine in glasses, they hid a lot of her face. Contacts would remedy that – bring out her true beauty.

Drake glanced at his watch. "My time is up. I have to get going."

"You're busy today, huh?"

"Yes. I have several job interviews this afternoon—need to hire more maintenance techs for my team."

"Okay. Thanks for having lunch with me again."

"Thanks for hanging out with me. Again."

Drake reached for a handshake. She accepted it.

"I'll see you later," he said.

"Yes. Later."

* * *

As Drake was preparing to leave the hotel, he stopped by the front desk.

"Hey, Jojo."

"Hey. Should I just reserve a room for you here?"

"*Ha ha*. No. I have a cozy, four-bedroom house that's perfect from me. This hotel is nice but it ain't *that* nice."

"There's no place like home."

"You got that right. Ay, look—I need you to do me a favor."

"What kind of favor?"

"Lavina needs a gown for the launch party on Saturday. Do you think you could squeeze some time in your schedule to take her to a few stores?"

Joelle didn't respond. She only flashed a pleasant smile.

"What is it, Jojo?"

"You like her, don't you?"

"What gave it away? The fact that I'm here every day or that I'm asking you to help her find a dress?"

"Aren't you sweet...didn't know you had it in you, Drake. Aw..."

"If you pinch my cheeks I'm telling Giovanni."

Joelle laughed. "I should be able to sneak out of here late Friday morning to take her. It'll be fun."

"Good. Thanks, Jojo."

Chapter 9

On Thursday, Drake was at the hotel with one of his workers to assist Lavina with the lights. When they were done, they stood beneath a sky of miniature bulbs that hung from wall to wall – thousands of little lights that had the room already looking like she wanted it.

"Wow," Lavina said, in awe. "It's just as I imagined it would be."

Drake watched, pleased with the happiness on her face, glad he played a part in it. From all he'd gathered about her, she didn't come across this kind of happiness often, even though she should have with the kind of work she did. She should've found this kind of fulfillment every day. He knew why that was a challenge for her, but she seemed oblivious to it. Whatever the case, looking at the lights equaled a victory for her because she was getting what she wanted.

Drake took a step closer to her. "Is this the effect you were going for?"

"It is. I love it," she said elated.

"Good. Hey, by the way, Joelle's taking you shopping on Friday."

"She is?"

"Yeah. She'll probably talk to you about it today."

"Now, I'm actually looking forward to this weekend. It's going to be amazing," she said adjusting her glasses and looking up at the lights again. "Thank you for helping me."

"You're welcome, Lavina." The corner of his mouth lifted into a half-smile. He liked Lavina but something about her interaction with him was off. Usually, women threw themselves at him. Around these parts, the Lennox men ruled. If you were lucky enough to score a Lennox, you made it. And even though this was the case, he'd been extremely picky with women – weeding out gold diggers along with the overly needy ones who lacked ambition. After that, only a few remained. Still, they didn't capture his interest. But Lavina had. She was an anomaly – a reserved entrepreneur. He wanted her to be more forthcoming with what she wanted. He wanted to know for certain if he caught her interest the same way she caught his.

* * *

He had the same conversation with Remington later that afternoon. He had gone to his cousin's office seeking advice about a woman – something he'd never done before.

Remington said, "It sounds like you're already on the right path. You've been helping her with the launch party and you made yourself her date, but what have you done specifically to give her a clue that you're interested and not just being friendly?"

"Rem, I helped this girl hang three trillion lights earlier today."

Remington chuckled. "Look here's what I can tell you. I was friends with Emory for a long time before letting her know how I really felt about her. A *long* time. Looking back now, I wish I would have said something sooner—like maybe the same weekend we met. But I didn't. We eventually got together but don't make the same mistake I made, man. If I'd waited a little longer, I would've lost her and I wouldn't have my beautiful daughter."

Drake nodded. "But it's crazy, right? I've only known Lavina for the better part of a week and I feel a strong connection with this woman. I feel like I want the best for her. I want to protect her. I want her to be happy."

Remington smiled because he knew what this meant for his cousin even if he didn't fully understand what that meant. He said, "You must really like this girl. I don't recall you ever having a conversation with me about a woman."

"That's how I know I like her, and I think I know what I need to do now. Thanks, man," he said rushing for the door.

"Ay, where are you running off to, man?"

"I just had an idea. Thanks for the advice."

Chapter 10

Only ten more centerpieces and she'd be done with the table décor.

Only ten...

She paid careful attention to each vase. They were stuffed with clear marbles to give an ice effect and glitter-covered cotton balls to give a snow effect. Finally, she'd place light blue snowflake stickers on the stem of the vases.

Only ten more to go...

She glanced at the clock. It was a few minutes after eight. If she wasn't such a perfectionist, she would've been done by now. And she hadn't had a thing for dinner. Aleeta was supposed to be helping with the vases but claimed she was still editing a video. Lavina had asked her to bring some food but she hadn't brought over anything yet. So Lavina kept working, stuffed her mouth with plain potato chips and focused on getting the last remaining vases completed before nine.

She was about to start on a new one when she heard a knock at the door. Had Aleeta finally brought her some food? She sure hoped so.

She glanced through the peephole and saw Drake standing there with the bag. She opened the door.

"Drake?"

"Lavina?" he said amused, saying her name the same way she said his. Like a question.

"Wha-what are you doing here?"

"I figured you were in here killing yourself trying to get some last-minute stuff done so I brought you some dinner. Is that enough of an explanation for you to invite me in, or—?"

"Uh…" She chewed on her lip. "I reckon."

"You reckon?" he asked, stepping into the room. She had booked a one-bedroom suite. The kitchen and living room is where she'd obviously been working. Cotton balls, glitter, vases, boxes – the room looked like a small stationery factory.

"Let me clear a spot at the table," she said moving a cardboard box full of vases.

Drake placed the bag there then removed his coat before he started unpacking it.

"Is that from Bryson City Barbeque?"

"It is."

"Oh my gosh. You're my best friend right now!"

He chuckled. "Everybody loves Bryson City Barbecue."

"Especially the pulled pork. It's my favorite."

"Mine, too," he told her. "That's what I got—with slaw, fries and hush puppies on the side. Aren't you glad you let me in now? Do you still *reckon* that you let me in?" he teased.

"I was going to let you in, anyway. I was just surprised you were here."

She sat down while Drake served her a carryout container full of food. "Thank you."

"You're welcome."

She opened the box and began scarfing the food down something vicious. "OMG—so good," she mumbled.

"You should take more breaks."

"Can't. I have to finalize the decorations since I'll be with Joelle for most of the day tomorrow. Plus, when I want something done, I want it done." She took another bite of her sandwich while he watched.

He asked, "What else do you have to do?"

She threw up her index finger, grabbed a napkin to wipe her mouth and mumbled, "I have to finish the vases...and get them set up on the tables tomorrow. Early Saturday morning we have three-hundred silver, white and baby blue balloons being delivered. They'll all have long silver strings that'll make for an easy take-down after the party is over." She took a sip of water.

"Alternatively, I can buy a BB gun and shoot them all down," Drake said.

She laughed. Drank more water.

"Have I ever told you that you have a beautiful smile?" he asked.

"No. Thanks," she said glancing up, then quickly went back to eating.

"You're welcome."

* * *

When they finished their meals, he cleaned off the table, tossed the bag in the trash and asked, "What can I do to help?"

"You've done so much already, Drake. You've done *more* than enough."

"Yet, you still look overwhelmed," he told her. "I want to help you."

She smiled and frowned at the same time. "Are you sure?"

"I am. Now, what kind of girly stuff are we getting into tonight?"

"*Girly stuff.* You're funny."

"This *is* girly stuff. Men don't care about glitter and stickers."

"Which is why you should get out of here while you still can." She placed the box on the table.

"Nah. Put me to work. Use me, baby."

"Oh, jeez...okay. Before you came, I was working on placing snowflake stickers on these vases. I have nine more left. Do you think you can handle it?"

"Sounds easy enough. Sure. I got this," he said, popping his knuckles, then rolled his head around like he was working the kinks out of his neck.

Lavina removed a vase from the box and handed it to him, along with a sheet of stickers.

"I'll have these done in no time," he told her.

While he was busy with his assigned task, she was dropping marbles in the vases, then followed up with stuffing cotton balls on top, sprinkling in glitter.

She glanced up periodically to watch him work. He was putting his all into it. He said he wanted to help and he wasn't playing. But she hadn't expected this level of dedication and attention to detail. She was impressed to say the least.

"Joelle told me to be ready to go at eleven," she said.

"Good. You'll enjoy yourself with her. She's good people. By the way, The Lennoxes always support events like this so they'll all be here on Saturday."

"Really? They purchased tickets?"

"They did."

"That's awesome I'll get to meet more of the Lennox gang."

"Yep. We're a good bunch if I do say so myself."

"I know. People around here have a lot of respect for you all. And everybody knows Remington's story, of course—the way he raised his siblings after their mother abandoned them."

Drake nodded. He remembered how difficult it was but Remington kept it together – his sanity and his family. He said, "Real men show how *real* they are when things like that happen."

"Absolutely."

"It's sometimes easier to throw in the towel—at least that's what our brain wants us to believe. Like, let's take you for an example, Lavina."

"Me?" she asked gesturing to herself.

"Yes. *You*."

"I haven't thrown in the towel. I'm a hard worker."

"I'm not disputing that, but in a way, you've become lax."

"How do you figure?"

He took another vase from the box and said, "You've grown comfortable with sitting on the sidelines while Aleeta takes over *your* business."

Lavina's brows creased as she grew slightly offended. Why was he constantly bringing up Aleeta? Defending her friend, she responded, "Aleeta has helped me grow the business—"

"They're your products, Lavina," he asserted.

His eyes darkened as he cast them upon her, she noticed.

He continued, "Without the products, there is no business."

"True, but—"

"No buts. You need to get off the sidelines and start playing big."

She sighed heavily. She meant to internalize it, but it came out anyway.

"Why's that so hard for you?" he asked, pausing work to give her his full attention.

"I would be so uncomfortable doing that. I'm not outgoing like her. Or *you*. That's not who I am. I'm a creator. I—"

"Have you ever heard the saying, 'great things never came from comfort zones'?"

"Yes, but—"

"What about 'if you want something you've never had you have to do something you've never done'? And 'if it doesn't challenge you, it won't change you'?"

"I've heard all of those before."

"They're more than just words. When Remington first offered me the maintenance manager position at Lennox Enterprises, I was hesitant to take it even though I knew the ins and outs of it like the back of my hand. I was well qualified, but I kept asking myself *what if I screw up*? But then I asked myself, *what if I can get in there and rock it*? So, that's what I did. I took the job, even took some supplemental courses to improve my computer skills and organizational skills, but I didn't turn it down. I rocked it. You should do the same, even if you have to take some speaking classes or do some other activity that will get you out of that shell. It's a beautiful world out here, sweetie, and you can't see it beneath a rock. Besides, you're too beautiful to be hidden."

She smiled. He made some good points to issues she'd already been thinking about for a while. Maybe the time had come to listen to her gut and the good advice she was getting from her new Lennox friend.

With his fine self...

* * *

It was past eleven when the vases were completed only because Drake took his sweet time – working intentionally slow to extend his time with her.

Lavina put all vases back into the box then said, "I'm glad that's done."

"I guess I'll get out of your hair now," he said standing. Stretching. He slid into his jacket. "I have more interviews in the morning. Gotta wash all this glitter off of me before fools think I'm soft."

Lavina giggled as she followed him to the door. "Please. Glitter or no glitter—first look at you and they'll know you ain't for play."

He pulled the door open, then stepped right outside of it. Lavina kept her feet against the door so it didn't close since she didn't have her room key in her pocket.

"Thanks for all of your help again," she said.

"Not a problem."

"I'm sure I'll see you at some point tomorrow," she said.

"Yes, I'm sure, and I'm looking forward to it already," he told her.

Drake reached for her hand although he preferred much more – a hug, kiss – anything other than the connection of a handshake.

Lavina extended her hand to his and when their hands touched, she shook his.

Felt the spark, like always.

The fire.

The connection.

The vibe.

It was when she decided she wanted much more than a handshake. She wanted him close. She released his hand and closed her arms around him. What a feeling it was to have him so close. She could hold him this way forever but she had to release him for now, didn't she?

As they parted, she brushed a kiss across his cheek. Her eyes held his as their lips sat inches apart.

She licked her lips.

His eyes weighed heavily on them.

She nervously bit down on her bottom lip.

Why had she done a thing like that?

He pulled her glasses from her face, nudged her chin up slightly then closed the distance between them by taking a soft kiss from her lips. He pulled back, looked at her – to feel her out. If he was reading her correctly, she could handle much more of what he'd been giving her. So, he gave her more.

Still kissing, he walked her back into the room. The door closed and she found herself sandwiched between the hotness of a Lennox and the steel door along with everlasting strokes of his tongue – strokes that made her gasp for air and sanity. He was taking all of it – even cupped her face in his hands so he could angle her head just right, sending his tongue to her throat.

Lavina could just die. She'd been kissed before, a long time ago, but never like this. Drake was so far in her mouth she couldn't tell whose tongue belonged to who. You know you're done for when a man is able to kiss the sense right out of you and that's what he was doing – kissing her logical thoughts away to the point of making her question whether or not she ever had any.

Slowly – meticulously slow – he pulled his tongue from her mouth then left little kisses all around her lips. Then, with his lips touching hers, he said, "I like you."

"I like you, too, Drake," she said. She wasn't quite sure how the words had left her mouth, but she said them.

"I'll see you tomorrow."

He took a final kiss, then pulled the door open to exit a second time, walking toward the elevator.

Aleeta stepped out of her room, looked across the hallway and saw Lavina smiling from ear-to-ear as she watched Drake near the elevator. She rolled her eyes, knowing her friend hadn't seen her then after sucking in a breath of deception, she said, "Hey, you're still up."

She invited herself into Lavina's room. "Yeah," she said. "I just finished up some work."

"Did I just see Drake Lennox leaving here?"

"You did. He brought me some dinner and I'm glad he did because you never showed up."

"Girl, you know how it is when you're in the middle of recording."

"Actually, I don't know how it is."

"You so crazy," she giggled. "Anyway, what

did he want?"

"Who?" Lavina asked.

"Drake."

"Oh. Nothing. He asked to be my date for the party on Saturday."

"Did he?" Aleeta asked, darting her head back as if she couldn't believe it.

Lavina looked at her. "Yeah. Why do you say it like it's hard to believe?"

"Because it is. I knew he was no good the moment I saw him."

"What are you talking about?" Lavina asked testily.

Aleeta responded, "He asked to be my date and I turned him down."

Lavina couldn't believe what she'd heard. "He...he asked to...to be your date?"

"Girl, yes. I stay fanning men up off of me."

"When?" Lavina asked trying to keep a straight face like the news she'd heard from Aleeta wasn't jarring and hurtful.

Aleeta shrugged. "I don't remember when exactly. Earlier this week, I suppose. I turned him down, though—must be why he asked you."

Like I'm second-best, Lavina thought. *If you can't have the beauty queen, settle for the beauty queen's bestie in hopes of one day landing the beauty queen's affection.* Is that what this was? Drake wasn't her man. She realized that but still, she thought he liked her. Genuinely. But here she was playing second-best in Aleeta shadows, yet again.

"But enough about that buster," Aleeta said. "Men will be men. Hey, you want me to get you a gown for Saturday? I saw this orange-sherbet-colored one that will look so good on you."

"Orange sherbet? Like orange mixed with vanilla ice cream...?"

"Yeah."

"Why would I wear a dress that doesn't even go with the color scheme? The colors are blue, white and silver."

"So what? You can wear whatever color you want," Aleeta said.

"What color is your dress?" Lavina asked her.

"Silver."

"So, you're wearing a pretty silver dress and you want me to walk around looking like low-fat ice cream."

"I'm the host, Vina. I have to look the part."

"And I'm a nobody so I have to *not* look the part. Is that what you're saying?"

"Girl, you'll be fine."

"Really, because I can't figure out how an orange dress is supposed to look with my red glasses."

"It's a pretty dress," Aleeta said sternly. "Nobody's gonna notice your glasses, anyway."

"Here's a suggestion," Lavina said, "Since the dress is so pretty, you wear it. Now can you leave so I can finally go to bed?"

"Wow, okay. Somebody's a little irritated. Must be on your cycle..."

"You're going to be *on the floor* if you don't

83

get out of my room."

Aleeta walked to the door, snatched it open and bounced. When it latched closed, Lavina secured the deadbolt and took a quick shower before getting into bed. It was already midnight and she couldn't sleep all because of what Aleeta had said about Drake. How could he...?

How could he claim to like her so much, yet ask to accompany her best friend to the party? Was he playing her? Stringing her along so he could get close to Aleeta? What were his true intentions?

Chapter 11

Joelle opened the door to the boutique, excited about being away from the lodge. But why did she seem more excited than Lavina? This shopping excursion was for her after all, yet she seemed less than thrilled.

She didn't know much about Lavina – but she knew Drake liked her. That told her all she needed to know about her right there. Drake had always been picky with women. Said he was the type of guy to take his time and find a good relationship instead of wasting his time, money and energy on a bunch of *possibles*. So he must've seen something in Lavina and she had an idea what it was.

Lavina was a sweet girl. A little on the quiet side, but nevertheless, she was sweet. Drake was the opposite – not the opposite of sweet because, like all the Lennox men, he was a complete gentleman. He was the opposite of her because he wasn't quiet. He was a businessman. Charming. Had that signature Lennox kilowatt smile and a sense of humor that women couldn't get enough of. She was sure it's what had hooked Lavina.

"You said you're looking for a light blue gown, right?" Joelle asked.

"Yes. Light blue or at least some variation of blue."

Joelle frowned. "The party isn't overwhelming you is it? I see you've been working hard all morning to get everything perfect. I took a peep inside the banquet room. It looks lovely. You nailed the winter theme and the lights—looks like something off of a movie set."

"Thanks, Joelle."

"You're welcome. Hey, are you okay?"

"Yeah...yeah. I'm...um—" Lavina froze as her eyes landed on the perfect dress. A long, light blue gown with a hint of shimmer and lace shoulder straps. It was perfect for a party she no longer wanted to attend. Go figure...

"Lavina?"

She blinked out of a trance and looked at Joelle. "Oh, sorry. My eyes landed on this beautiful dress," she said reaching for it, "But I'm not even sure if I want to go to the launch party now."

"After all the hard work you've done. Why not?"

"I just—I don't know." She sighed.

"What happened?"

"It's...it's Drake."

"What about him?"

"He asked to be my date for the party, then last night, Aleeta told me he asked her, too and since she turned him down, he asked me. I'm so tired of living in her shadow. Of always being *second*-best. She's always been prettier. More outgoing. Of course he would've asked her out."

"Uh, first off, Drake cannot stand the sight of Aleeta. No offense, I know she's your best friend and all, but she's not all that *friendly* and I seriously doubt if Drake asked to be her plus-one. No way."

"Well, that's what Aleeta told me last night."

"And you trust and believe what she said because you also told me on the drive over here that she tried to convince you to wear an ugly, sherbet-orange dress? Maybe, *just maybe,* your friend isn't that much of a *friend* after all, Lavina."

"She has her ways, but why would she lie about Drake asking to be her date for the party?"

"Simply because she knows Drake is interested in you and she can't stand it or him. You don't think she's noticed him hanging around here, eating lunch with you, helping you with the decorations and all that? She's seen it. And she's jealous." Joelle took the dress from the rack. "Come on. You have to try it on. You're *going* to this party and you're going to look fabulous!"

In the dressing room, Lavina changed into the gown then stepped out so Joelle could see the fit of the size ten dress. She looked at herself in the mirror, pleased with how the dress conformed to her figure.

"It looks lovely," Joelle said excitedly. "You look like the belle of the ball and you're not even there yet."

Lavina turned around to see the opened backside of the dress via one of the angled mirrors. It was elegant and she had to admit she felt pretty in it. She shouldn't let Drake, Aleeta or anyone else prevent her from celebrating this accomplishment. Mountain View Beauty was *her* company, *her* products, and it was doggone time she started acting like it.

"Do you like it?" Joelle asked.

"I do. I love it. I think I'll go ahead and buy it."

"You don't want to check any other stores first?"

"Nope. I'm not big on shopping. Plus, I doubt if I'd find anything better than this one."

"Okay, then. I guess that's it for dress shopping. You want to grab some lunch before we head back to the lodge since we have time?"

"Sure."

"What's your preference?"

Lavina shrugged. "Don't have one."

"Then let's go to Island Street Deli. They have a good soup selection around this time of the year. As cold as it is today, I can go for some hot soup."

"That's fine," Lavina said. Around the same

time, she got a text message from Drake.

Drake: Can I take you to lunch?

Lavina rolled her eyes. *Why don't you take Aleeta to lunch?*

A few minutes later after they'd parked on the street in front of the deli, she decided to message him back.

Lavina: I have plans.
Drake: *sad face emoji*
Drake: What about dinner?
Lavina: I'll have plans then, too. It's the night before launch. Super busy
Drake: Then at what point can I see you today?
Lavina: Why do you want to see me at all?

She put her phone back into her purse when they crossed the salt-treated sidewalk before stepping inside the deli.

Joelle spoke to several workers, then Lavina noticed she was greeted by the manager.

"You must come here a lot," Lavina said.

"I used to work here."

"Before you started working at the lodge?"

"Well," Joelle said as they walked to a table. "I was working at the lodge first, but the manager at the time was a plum-dumb idiot and I couldn't stand it anymore, so I quit."

Lavina's eyes brightened. "You quit?"

"I did, then Remington wanted me back, so he sent his brother to convince me to stay."

Lavina smiled. "Giovanni."

"Yes. Girl, he was a pain in the butt to deal with, but then he grew on me. He's a lot like Drake. You can definitely tell they're related."

Ah, so that's how you and Giovanni got together...

"Hey, Joelle!" Vanessa, a waitress Joelle used to work with, said walking to her table.

"Hey, Vanessa!"

Vanessa leaned down to give her a quick hug and then Joelle said, "This is my friend, Lavina."

"Hi," Lavina said.

"Me and Vanessa used to work together," Joelle told her.

"Yeah, that's before she got married and forgot about us," Vanessa said.

"Aw—I didn't forget about y'all. I just have my hands full at the lodge now."

"I'm just teasing you, girl. What can I get y'all to drink?"

"Water for me," Joelle said.

"Me, too," Lavina told her. "And I think I want to try the chicken and rice soup."

"I think I will, too," Joelle said.

"All right, ladies. I'll be right back."

"Excuse me for a moment, Lavina," Joelle said taking out her phone. "I need to check in and make sure everything is kosher at the lodge."

"No problem," Lavina said because she'd use the time to check her phone, too. She saw some texts from Drake.

Drake: Why do you 'think' I want to see you?

Drake: I enjoy your company. Thought you knew that.

And then...

Drake: Are you there?

Lavina thought about responding, but imagining him asking Aleeta to the launch party was playing with her head. So she put her phone back into her purse and enjoyed eating soup and getting to know Joelle.

"How long have you and Aleeta been friends?" Joelle asked.

"A long time...since we were in third grade."

"It's insane how different you two are. It's like night and day."

"I know. Everybody says that."

"But you know what you don't want?"

"What's that?" Lavina asked.

"You don't want to be so close to someone who doesn't support you in the way they should. Do you know what I mean by that?"

"I think so, but like I told Drake, Aleeta's always been there."

"But how much did she actually do to help you prepare the ballroom for the launch party tomorrow? I saw you doing most of the work. Every time I saw her, she was on her laptop. She didn't even help you and Drake hang the lights. What exactly did she do? It's almost like you're her assistant and you do all the heavy lifting while she goes off and plays pretty for the cameras."

"I know. You're right. She's just so much more of a social butterfly."

"Doesn't matter. It's your company. Earlier, you said you felt like you were living in Aleeta's shadow. Well, it's time to get out of that. I know how it is to let things hold you back from living. I know the feeling all too well."

Joelle took a sip of water, then continued, "I don't know if you know this and I don't share it with everyone, but I lost my family in a house fire. My parents and my sister. I barely made it out."

"Oh my gosh. I'm so sorry."

"Thanks." Joelle took a moment to collect her thoughts after thinking about her family. It always pained her to think of them. She cleared her throat and said, "Anyway, I say that to let you know I often think about them and my sister. She was younger than me. I think about who she would've become if she was still here, but she's not here. I'm here. *You're* here, and while you're here, Lavina—while you still have breath in your body—you should live your life. Don't play small. Play big—as big and as fabulous as that banquet room is for your launch party tomorrow."

Lavina smiled. "You're right. Thanks, Joelle. I appreciate you sharing your story."

"No problem. Now, what's this new product you're unveiling. I need something for these fine lines," she said pointing to the area beneath her eyes.

"Whatever. You don't have any lines. You're beautiful."

"So are you, and speaking of that, are we going to the hair salon?"

"No. I have an appointment tomorrow for hair and nails."

"Good, and one more thing...do you have a different pair of glasses? I don't think those red ones will do anything to make your overall look pop."

"I'm wearing contacts."

"Cool. You're going to look so hot, Drake won't be able to keep his eyes off of you."

Lavina cracked a smile. She wasn't sure if she wanted that kind of attention from him. Not anymore.

Chapter 12

Back at the hotel, Lavina carried her gown up to her room. When she stepped off the elevator, she saw Drake standing by the door to her room – looking like a dream.

Great. After a fantastic day, now this...

She was so nervous, she could hardly put one foot in front of the other. Did he have to look so fine today? He rocked a pair of jeans, boots, that bad-boy leather jacket again and a black baseball cap. And to think a guy like him was interested in her...

She must've bumped her head. Actually, she *had* bumped her head and it was all *his* fault. Still, that wishful thinking kicked in – the kind of mind-wandering that made every girl think the hottest guy in the room wanted *her*. But if she was being real, men like Drake Lennox were the upper echelon of the male species that women like Aleeta attracted on a daily basis with no effort – even with her stank attitude.

"Hi," he said as she got closer. "Did you find

a dress?"

"I did," she said, stopping in front of him. She wasn't about to open the door and let him inside to attack her with those deadly lips of his – not after what Aleeta had told her. But was there any truth to it? Most likely there was. When had a guy ever dissed Aleeta to talk to her? Um...how 'bout *never*!

"How was your shopping trip with Jojo?"

"It was cool."

Drake nodded, then took a hard look at her. She was different. Something was wrong. He could sense that via the text message exchange they had earlier in the day. He asked, "Is everything okay?"

"Yes. Everything's fine. If you would excuse me, I need to get some things done for the party."

"Wow. Okay. Uh...all right. I'll see you later, then."

"About that—I'm not sure if that's a good idea. I think I need to go alone."

"Why?"

"It's nothing personal, Drake. It's just business," she said swiping the key to unlock the door. "I'll see you around."

She hurriedly stepped inside before he could ask any further questions, hung the gown in the closet then sat on the bed with her head hanging low. It was nice to entertain the thought of him having a real interest in her while it lasted, but deep down, she knew it wasn't real. After all, why would Drake choose the dorky girl in glasses over her hot best friend?

* * *

Drake was tempted to knock on the door and get a further explanation as to why she was giving him the cold shoulder, but he decided to give her room to breathe. Maybe she was stressed out about the launch. He didn't want to cause any further stress for her. He only wanted to help, but she hadn't given him the opportunity to do that.

Down in the lobby, he saw Joelle staring at the computer screen while typing so fast, her brain probably couldn't keep up with her fingers.

"Hey, girl."

She had on her headset, gesturing for him to give her a minute. When she was done with the call, she said, "Hey. What's up?"

"How did shopping go?"

"It went good. Real good. Lavina found a pretty dress at the first boutique we went to, then we grabbed some lunch."

"So, everything went fine, then."

"Yeah. Why? Something wrong?"

"I ran into her in the hallway by her room and she gave me a shoulder that was so cold I feel like I need a bigger jacket. That's what makes me think something happened."

"Oh. Um..."

"What happened, Jo?"

"Lavina was a little upset with you and if this

is true, so am I!"

"If what's true?"

She explained, "Aleeta went to Lavina's room last night. Lavina told Aleeta you were her date for the party. Aleeta said you asked her *first,* but she turned you down, making it seem like the only reason you asked Lavina is because Aleeta turned you down."

"That's a lie," Drake said frowning. "I wouldn't take Aleeta to McDonald's—let alone a party."

Joelle chuckled. "I knew it was a lie when I heard it, but can you see how Lavina could easily think this was true? In her mind, she has this inflated image of Aleeta being *soo* much prettier, so much *better* than her to the point that she believes Aleeta would've been your first choice for the party."

"Okay, then," Drake said, raising his shoulders. "There you have it."

"No. You can't leave her thinking the worst. Go back up to Lavina's room and tell her Aleeta lied."

Drake shook his head. "Nope. Not gon' do it."

"Why are you being stubborn, Drake?"

"All week I've been trying to warn Lavina about her so-called friend. If she can't see how shady that girl is on her own, then ain't no sense in me or anybody else trying to convince her. I'm out."

Drake walked out into the elements – light snow falling onto his head. When he climbed up into his truck and started it, the flakes became thicker and heavier – that wet, nasty snow that kids use to make snowmen and start snowball fights. He turned on the wipers, hit the defrost button for the windows and just sat there, watching the snow fall. He wanted to go back into the hotel, tell Lavina the truth, but what was the use, especially since she would continue being loyal and making excuses for someone who didn't deserve it?

Chapter 13

Lavina got up early, went to the hair salon and got her curly strands straightened. She then went to get her nails done in blue and silver to match her dress. And speaking of her dress – it looked ten times better now that she'd had her hair and nails done to match. Now, she was trying to put on some makeup.

Ugh, maybe I should've put the makeup on before the dress. I'm so bad at this...

After a tap at the door, she dropped the eyeliner pencil into the sink bowl and went to see who it was. She saw Joelle through the peephole, dressed beautifully in a white, knee-length dress and white heels.

She opened the door and said, "Wow. Look at you, Joelle, looking pretty in all your white."

"Just a lil' something I came up with."

"With a body like that, you can pull anything off," Lavina commented.

"Girl, please. You're the one with the body now that we can see it. You are *wearing* that dress."

"Thank you," Lavina said.

"I came up here to see if you needed some help."

"Do you think you can help me with my makeup?"

"Of course!" Joelle said eagerly. As soon as the door closed behind her, she was in the bathroom, applying foundation on a face that had no blemishes. Lavina could've gone barefaced and still looked like a model. She told her as much.

Lavina said, "Thanks. It's funny how other people can look at you and see beauty and then when you look at yourself, all you see are flaws."

"That's because we're our own worst critics," Joelle said. "Plus, these makeup companies have to stay in business somehow, so they make people feel vulnerable—like you *need* to wear makeup. I know this girl that won't leave her house unless she's fully made up."

"Wow."

"Then there are women like you with a dreamy complexion and cheekbones to die for." She added some shimmer and highlights to make the bone structure of Lavina's face stand out. She filled in her brows, then brushed them with a small eyebrow brush.

"What color do you want on your eyelids?"

"I'm thinking a bluish-purple combo with some glitter eyeshadow."

"Okay. I got you," she said, scanning the

palette for the colors she wanted. "You look so different without your glasses."

"I know...and to think Aleeta told me to wear them..."

"Oh. Did she really?" Joelle asked. She was about ready to choke Aleeta.

"She did."

Joelle applied the last few brushstrokes of purple and blue, then began to blend them in. "You know what—it's not my place to get involved in this kind of stuff but this has been bothering me all night."

"What's that?"

"I talked to Drake yesterday. He said he didn't ask Aleeta anything about going with her to the party, Lavina. Aleeta lied."

The knock at the door kept Lavina from replying. She said, "Let me see who that is," and walked there. When she opened the door, there stood Aleeta. She watched her friend's mouth fall open as she looked at her from head to toe.

"Wha...wha...where...where are your glasses?" Aleeta stammered. She looked puzzled and shocked.

"I'm not wearing glasses today. I have my contacts in."

"Oh."

Aleeta looked at her hair. It was flat-ironed silky straight, hanging down her back and framing her face. And her makeup was done to perfection along with her nails, her toes – what in the world? She'd been transformed into a princess.

Joelle came out of the room with a silver tiara and said, "Lavina, you *have* to wear this for the finishing touch." She placed it on Lavina's head and adjusted the pins to position it in place.

"Wait—you can't wear a tiara," Aleeta said, frowning. "*I'm* wearing a tiara."

Joelle grinned. "Are you serious? You say that like she needs your permission. You can both wear tiaras."

"I—this—I don't understand," Aleeta said.

"What don't you understand?" Lavina asked.

"I thought we agreed *I'd* be the star of the company."

Lavina's face scrunched up. "The *star*? No, we agreed you'd be the person who does the videos, whose face is on ads because you were the *pretty* one—the *outgoing* one who could convince people to buy the products. You've always kept me in the background like I wasn't good enough. You tried to get me to wear an orange dress with red glasses tonight and if that wasn't bad enough, you lied and said Drake asked to go with you to the party because you knew he wanted to go with me."

Aleeta rolled her eyes. "So what?"

Joelle said, "Let me step out. I'll see you later, Lavina." She *had* to step out before she choked Aleeta. Somebody needed to yank that weave off her head and beat her tail with it. Maybe then, she could think straight.

When Joelle exited, Lavina said, "*So what?* That's all you have to say after you lied?"

"Whatever. I've done a lot for this company."

"So have I! They're *my* products, Aleeta—every last single one of them. You haven't come up with anything." Lavina brought her hands to her temple. Unbelievable! How'd she let it get this far? "If you don't start treating me with some respect, I'll take my products and start my own company."

Aleeta rolled her eyes. "You're being extremely *extra* right now."

"Okay then. Since I'm so *extra*, I'm done. After the launch party is over, so is this business relationship. I can totally do this without you. I just needed a little push. A little confidence—you know—the very thing you *didn't* want me to have. Now, get out of my room."

Aleeta glared at her.

Lavina yelled, "Get out!"

Aleeta grunted then left.

Lavina smiled and mumbled, "Good riddance." She'd finally stood up for herself to the person she'd least expected she'd have to.

She walked to the mirror, checked her makeup, brushed her hair into place again as if it was needed, then slid into a pair of silver, glittery heels.

And now it was showtime!

When Lavina stepped into the ballroom, a gasp came over the crowd. Most of the people there, bloggers, media, even customers had always seen her in nothing more than a pantsuit and glasses but here she was stunning the crowd while Aleeta stood in the shadows for a change.

Lavina walked over to Aleeta and asked, "Are you going to welcome everyone or—?"

Aleeta crossed her arms and said, "Why don't you do it—you know—since you're going to *run your own company* and all?" She was certain she had Lavina backed into a corner since she knew Lavina wasn't one for the spotlight.

Lavina smiled, pulled in a deep breath and said, "I have to learn how to do this one day. May as well be today."

Aleeta looked puzzled as Lavina made her way to the stage. Lavina took a moment to look around at everyone – at the banquet room that looked just as she envisioned it. The white, silver and blue balloons lining the perimeter of the room. The string lights floating across the ceiling. The white tablecloths. The vases she'd worked hard to make. The silver grab bags. The champagne bars – two of them. This was the best launch party in Mountain View Beauty's history.

Her nerves were starting to get the best of her when she realized she had to do more than stand here. Everyone was still socializing, talking, networking. She had to somehow get people's attention.

She tapped on the microphone with her index finger and said, "Good afternoon everyone."

The crowd slowly quieted, then all eyes were on her. "I—" She paused. Did it just get hot in winter wonderland, or was it just her? She could feel a line of sweat run down the center of her back. "Hello. I just wanted to uh—"

She nervously chewed her lip. In her mind, she imagined rocking the mic, being a good host but it didn't translate that way as she looked at all the eyes beaming back at her. She scanned the crowd until her eyes locked in on one guest in particular – Drake Lennox – wearing a gray suit. From a distance, she could see a twinkle in his eyes. He smiled then patted his chest, signaling her to speak from her heart.

After the vote of confidence, she gave it another attempt. She said, "I'm grateful that you all could be here this afternoon. This launch has been a long time coming. As you know, Mountain View Beauty hasn't unveiled a new product in two years. I think that's what makes this one so special. I didn't want to rush it. I wanted to take my time and get it just right and that's what I've done. Later, we'll have the big reveal but for now, I want you to fill up on appetizers. We'll have dinner in about an hour. Thank you."

The crowd applauded and she quickly exited the stage, heart pounding, but still, she was grateful that she did it.

Now, she needed a glass of champagne.

She walked to a drink station, grabbed a glass and guzzled half of it down.

"Hi."

She looked to the left and up at the tall gentleman standing next to her. She knew he was a Lennox just by his features, but had no clue which Lennox this was since they all looked so much alike.

"Hi."

"I'm Remington Lennox," he said extending his hand to her.

Her eyes widened like she was talking to a celebrity. In this neck of the woods, the Lennoxes *were* celebrities.

"I'm Lavina Nelson. It's nice to meet you," she said shaking his hand.

"You as well. My wife raves about your products."

"Are you serious?"

"I am."

"Thank you. I'm honored that you're all here."

"We like to support our own."

"That's wonderful."

Remington took a look around and said, "You've done a brilliant job on this launch. Did you hire a party planner?"

"No. I did most of this on my own. Your cousin Drake helped me tremendously. In fact, if it wasn't for him, I wouldn't have these lights," she said looking up above her head. "And I wouldn't have gotten up on that stage."

"Is that so?"

"Yeah."

"That's interesting."

"Why do you say that?"

"I noticed you've been staying away from him since you made your grand entrance."

"Oh..." she said, surprised he actually paid

attention to that. How did he know anything about the two of them unless Drake had said something? "Yeah...um...it's kind of a long story."

"Let me tell you something about my cousin, Lavina. He's about his business."

"I know."

"He doesn't date much."

"No?"

"No. He values his time because he knows, just as well as you and I, that time is money."

"Absolutely."

"So, you tell me why Drake has worked part-time all this week—the first time he's ever done so since taking the managerial role."

She knew the answer to that. He worked part-time because he was busy helping her all week. Spending time with her, roasting marshmallows, helping her with the décor and doing whatever else he saw fit to assist.

"That wasn't rhetorical.," Remington said. "Tell me."

"Um...because...he likes me."

Remington smiled just barely. "Go talk to him."

"I would, but—"

"No worries. He doesn't hold grudges." Remington winked at her then walked off.

Lavina tossed back the rest of her drink, hoping to scrounge up some liquid courage, but if she could get on stage and talk in front of a crowd of two-hundred people, surely she could pull one man aside for a quick apology, right?

She honed in on his location. He was

standing by the Lennox section where their family had gathered. As he approached, he said, "You looked like a pro up there."

She flashed a half-smile, not believing him, but accepting the compliment anyway. "Thanks."

"Who's your friend, Drake?" Davina asked loudly.

He looked at Davina and watched her brows raise. She was the youngest of the Lennox siblings – the one who liked to stir the pot because she had no business of her own unless flirting with Corbin LeBlanc was *business.*

"This is my friend, Lavina," Drake said. He turned to Lavina and said, "This is the Lennox crew. I saw you talking to Remington a moment ago. This is his wife, Emory."

"Hi," Emory said.

"Hi."

Drake continued, "And this is Kenton and his wife Lauren...Jessalyn and her husband Spencer."

Lavina waved at them.

"You know Giovanni and Joelle already and that sneaky girl right there in the black dress is Davina."

"Nice to meet you all," Lavina said.

"You look amazing," Jessalyn told her.

"I have to thank Joelle for that. She did my makeup and helped me pick out this dress."

"Wow. I didn't know you could do makeup like that, Joelle," Davina said.

"It was a piece of cake, and Lavina's got the

face for it."

Drake turned to look at her again. *Boy did she ever...*

This was the first time he'd seen her without the glasses – well outside of the time he removed them when he kissed her. He thought she was beautiful before but when she first walked into the room, the sight of her, her presence, her energy nearly knocked him off his feet. This was the same woman he'd been kickin' it with all week. Laughing with. Sharing meals and roasting marshmallows with. Decorating the ballroom with. And now, she'd transformed into a chocolate princess.

She looked at him, catching his hard, amber gaze on her and said, "I need to talk to you about what happened the other day. I owe you an apology."

"Lavina—"

"You've been trying to warn me all week, and I wasn't listening to you. I guess I had to see it for myself."

"Lavina—"

"No, let me say this before I lose the nerve," she told him. "I was wrong. I didn't give you a chance to explain last night," she said, her voice weak. "And I'm sorry."

The Lennox family was all ears – not that they were trying to be nosey, but she was standing at their table.

Drake took her by the hand and escorted her to the lobby. Standing near one of the tropical plants, he said, "You know if you want to talk to me, it can happen in private. Not in front of people."

"I know. I just—I—I didn't—um—"

"Lavina," he said touching her shimmering cheek, his thumb lightly tracing those cheekbones he adored.

She looked up at him. "Yes?"

"By *see it for yourself*, I assume you're referring to Aleeta."

"Yes. I confronted her about what she said— about you asking her to come here with you tonight—and it was a lie."

"I'm glad you found that out, but what would make you think I'd ask her out when I'm totally, completely, one-hundred percent feeling you?"

She shied away from his eyes and his question. Then she looked at him – was all set to respond when he dipped his head and captured her fuchsia-tinted, soft lips. Her pulse quickened – she nearly lost the ability to breathe when she felt his tongue stroke hers, leaving her dizzy with desire.

And that was just a kiss.

Was kissing supposed to leave her breathless. Was his mouth supposed to latch and suck on her lips? Was her spine supposed to tingle? Mind turn to mush? Was she supposed to forget where she was?

She looked around. *Where am I?*

"Lavina, are you all right?"

She blinked then focused her eyes on him. "Yes. I'm okay."

"You sure?"

"Yes. Um—you really like me, huh?"

"I do, and yes, I want to get to know you. Your family. Your idiosyncrasies. Your—everything. I want to know everything there is to know because I like you and no one else."

"Okay," she said all smiles. "I like you, too."

"Then I think you should kiss me with those pretty lips of yours.

"Oh, really?"

"Yes. Really."

After the smile fell from her face, she captured his lips, interlocking hers with his and enjoying the feeling of his arms around her. She freed herself and closed her arms around his neck while they smooched in the hallway – his head moving to the left, hers to the right interchangeably.

"Ahem," they heard close to them.

Lavina pulled her lips away from his and looked for the source. Her friend Aleeta was standing there.

"Hey," Lavina said.

"Hey," Aleeta responded. She sounded angry. Who sounds angry when they said *hey*?

"I'll give you two a minute," Drake said. He returned to the ballroom.

Lavina looked at Aleeta and crossed her arms. "What's up?"

"Did you really threaten to dissolve our company?"

"Aleeta, if you're not here to apologize—"

"Apologize for *what*?" she snapped.

"For the way you've been treating me. You're supposed to be my friend, my *best* friend, and you're perfectly fine with me being in the background while you run this company like these are *your* products. These aren't your products. And you know what? I thought we were supposed to be partners, but we're not partners. We've never been partners. I'm the CEO and you're the person who's good at marketing, so going forward, that's what your new role will be—VP of Marketing—while I take this company in the direction I want it to go in—including approving the marketing campaigns before they run."

"Why would I agree to that?" she asked.

"Because if you don't, I will dissolve the company and take my products with me. Then you can start your own company with your own products—oh, wait, that's right—you don't have any."

Aleeta rolled her eyes.

"Oh, and one more thing—I like Drake and he likes me, so can you try to be a little cordial to him and his family."

"Okay. Anything else? *Boss*?"

Lavina smiled. "No. That'll be all for now."

Aleeta was fuming when she walked away but Lavina didn't care. She was finally taking control of her life and her company and it felt great.

* * *

After dinner, Lavina walked to the podium and said, "I hope everyone is having a great time this evening.

The crowd applauded.

She continued, "Today is a big day for Mountain View Beauty. We've been tight-lipped about our new products—yes, that's right I said *products*—but the time has come. This evening, Mountain View Beauty is releasing a new haircare line—a shampoo, a conditioner, a curl enhancer, and a creamy shea butter pomade—and they're all one-hundred percent natural. And that's not all. We haven't left out the men this time. We have a shampoo, conditioner and pomade for you as well. Tonight, we're giving full-size samples of both the men and women's products to everyone in attendance."

The crowd erupted with cheers and applause. Lavina had to wait until the commotion died down before saying, "Finally, I would like to say—um—when I started making products all the way back in college, I never imagined it would grow into what it is today, but I'm grateful for the support I've received from the community over the years and a very special man who, in one week's time, encouraged me step outside of my comfort zone." She flashed a warm smile to Drake, then closed with, "Thank you, everyone."

Lavina walked toward the stairs to exit the stage and saw Drake standing near the bottom. He extended his hand to hers to assist her down then said, "Congratulations, woman. You were phenomenal."

"Thank you."

"I want to know more about that *very special* man you were talking about."

"Um...let's see," she said putting her arms around his neck. "He's handsome, funny, he has a smile that makes my heart skip beats and he's just an overall, nice, charming guy."

"I wonder if he knows you're taken. Hmm..."

"I don't know."

"Then, you should tell him."

"I'm taken," she said, feeling Drake's arms circle around her, his large hands stroking the warm skin of her smooth, bare back. Without hesitation, he captured her mouth for a deeply satisfying, soul-stirring, captivating kiss beneath the cloud of lights they'd hung together. She couldn't wait for their relationship to grow, mature and become something much more. Could she handle a man like Drake? With all the confidence in the world, she knew she could. Could a man like Drake really like her? Yes, and he *did* like her. That, she no longer had to wonder about.

~ * ~

Enjoyed *Winter Wonder?* Please support the author by leaving a review. Also, subscribe to Tina's newsletter and be the first to know when the next new book hits the bookstores! Visit www.tinamartin.net

More about the Lennox Series:

Caught in the Storm with a Lennox (A Short Story Prequel to *Claiming You*)
BOOK 0
Remington Lennox and Emory McNeil (The Beginning)

Remington Lennox pretends to be in search of property in Atlanta when he supposedly stumbles across Emory's house after he's stranded in a snowstorm. She thinks he's a complete stranger, but he knows her...

———————

Claiming You (A Lennox in Love Novella)
BOOK 1
Remington Lennox and Emory McNeil

Emory McNeil is twenty-nine and was living a simple, modest life before she met Remington Lennox, a distinguished gentleman, who's a decade older than she is. Strictly friends for two years, their bond is strong, but everything changes when Remington feels like his brother is trying to steal her away from him.

———————

Making You My Business (A Lennox in Love Novella)
BOOK 2
Giovanni Lennox and Joelle Bannon

Giovanni's goal was to get Joelle Bannon to take her job back at Smoky Mountain Lodge, a hotel owned and operated by Lennox Enterprises. He didn't plan on falling in love.

Wishing That I Was Yours (A Lennox in Love Novella)
BOOK 3
Jessalyn Lennox and Spencer Wakefield

Jessalyn has hidden a crush with Spencer Wakefield (her brother's best friend) for over a decade. He's always been the man of her dreams, but will a relationship potentially screw up his friendship with her brothers?

Before You Say I Do (A Lennox in Love Novella)
BOOK 4
Kenton Lennox and Lauren Chandler

Lauren Chandler is back in Bryson City, North Carolina with her fiancé, Evan Kaizer, preparing for her engagement party. But her ex, Kenton Lennox, is always popping up in her way. And it doesn't help that the engagement party is being held at a resort owned by Lennox Enterprises.

Discover other books by Tina Martin:

St. Claire Series
*All books in this series are standalone novels and are full, complete stories. Read them in any order.

Royal
Ramsey
Romulus
Regal
Magnus
Monty
Honeymoon With a St. Claire (A follow-up to Monty)

Seasons of Love Novelettes
Hot Chocolate: A Winter Novelette
Spring Break: A Spring Novelette

The Boardwalk Bakery Romance
*This is a continuation series that must be read in order.

Baked With Love
Baked With Love 2
Baked With Love 3

The Marriage Chronicles
*This is a continuation series that must be read in order.

Life's A Beach
Falling Out
War, Then Love

The Blackstone Family Series
*All books in this series are standalone novels and are full, complete stories. Read them in any order.

Evenings With Bryson
Leaving Barringer
Forever Us: Barringer and Calista Blackstone (A short story follow-up to *Leaving Barringer*. You must read

Leaving Barringer before reading this short story)
The Things Everson Lost
Candy's Corporate Crush

A Lennox in Love Series
*All books in this series are standalone novellas and are full, complete stories. Read them in any order.

Claiming You
Making You My Business
Wishing That I Was Yours
Caught in the Storm with a Lennox (A Short Story Prequel to Claiming You)
Before You Say I Do

Mine By Default Mini-Series:
*This is a continuation series that must be read in order.

Been In Love With You, Book 1
When Hearts Cry, Book 2
You Belong To Me, Book 3
When I Call You Mine, Book 4
Who Do You Love?, Book 5
Forever Mine, Book 6

The Champion Brothers Series:
*All books in this series are standalone novels and are full, complete stories. Read them in any order.

His Paradise Wife
When A Champion Wants You
The Best Thing He Never Knew He Needed
Wives And Champions
The Way Champions Love
His By Spring
A Champion's Proposal

The Accidental Series:
*This is a continuation series that must be read in order.

Accidental Deception, Book 1

Accidental Heartbreak, Book 2
Accidental Lovers, Book 3
What Donovan Wants, Book 4

Dying To Love Her Series:
*This is a continuation series that must be read in order.

Dying To Love Her
Dying To Love Her 2
Dying To Love Her 3

The Alexander Series:
*Books 1-4 must be read in order. Books 5, 6,7 and can be read in any order as a standalone books.

The Millionaire's Arranged Marriage, Book 1
Watch Me Take Your Girl, Book 2
Her Premarital Ex, Book 3
The Object of His Obsession, Book 4
Dilvan's Redemption, Book 5
His Charity Challenge, Book 6 (Heshan Alexander and Charity Eason)
Different Tastes, Book 7 (An Alexander Spin-off novel. Tamera Alexander's Story)
As Long As We Got Love, Book 8 (Family Novel)

Non-Series Titles:
*Individual standalone books that are not part of a series.
Secrets On Lake Drive
Can't Just Be His Friend
The Baby Daddy Interviews
Just Like New to the Next Man
Falling Again
Vacation Interrupted
The Crush
Wasn't Supposed To Love Her
What Wifey Wants
Man of Her Dreams
Bae Watch

ABOUT THE AUTHOR

TINA MARTIN is the author of over 65 romance, romantic suspense and women's fiction titles and has been writing full-time since 2013. Readers praise Tina for her strong heroes, sweet heroines and beautifully crafted stories. When she's not writing, Tina enjoys watching movies, traveling, cooking and spending time with her family. She currently resides in Charlotte, North Carolina with her husband and two children.

You can reach Tina by email at **tinamartinbooks@gmail.com** or visit her website for more information at www.tinamartin.net.

Made in the USA
San Bernardino, CA
22 April 2020